The Brass Rainbow

*#2 in the Edgar Award-winning
Dan Fortune mystery series*

Dennis Lynds

Originally published under the pseudonym Michael Collins

The characters and events portrayed in this book are fictitious. Any similarities to real persons living or dead is coincidental and not intended by the author.

© 1969, 2011 by Gayle H. Lynds 2007 Revocable Trust
The Gayle H. Lynds 2016 Revocable Trust

Cover© 2015 Gayle Lynds
Cover Design: Shannon Raab
Cover Photographer:
Deklofenak/iStockphoto.com

All rights reserved. No part of this book may be reproduced, or stored in a retrieval system, or transmitted in any form or by any means, electronic, mechanical, photocopying, recording or otherwise, without express written permission of the publisher.

The Brass Rainbow e-book edition: 978-1-941517-02-4
The Brass Rainbow POD edition: 978-1-941517-03-1

For inquiries:
Gayle Lynds
P.O. Box 732
125 Forest Avenue
Portland, ME 04101-9998
www.DennisLynds.com

*To Ken Millar,
with thanks*

Acclaim for Dennis Lynds & His Novels

"The man who won the Mystery Writers of America award … has given readers another exceptional story." – *Parade of Books*

"Skillfully plotted with finely honed suspense." – *New York Times*

"[Lynds] is a writer to watch and above all to read." – *Ross Macdonald*

"A master of crime fiction." – *Ellery Queen Mystery Magazine*

"Smashing … leaves the reader breathless." – *Publishers Weekly*

"[Lynds's books are] filled with as much closely observed incident and detail as John O'Hara short stories." – *Wall Street Journal*

"First-class … suspenseful, character-rich, and absorbing." – *Kirkus Reviews*

"Some of the rawest, most unencumbered mystery writing extant in the genre." – *American Library Association*

"[He] carries on the Hammett-Chandler-Macdonald tradition with skill and finesse." – *Washington Post Book World*

"…combines superb characters and excellent plotting." – *ALA Booklist*

"... powerful writing." – *Library Journal*

"... engrossing and empathic." – *New York Daily News*

"... hot mystery writer whose novels have reached mainstream status. ..." – *San Diego Reporter*

"Collins is the Costa-Gavras of the PI world ... we might also call him the Captain Kirk of PI writers, boldly taking the genre where no colleague has gone before – and doing it so passionately that we can't help but sign on for the quest with him." – literary critic Francis M. Nevins, Jr.

"Lynds is a major contributor to the form, even a redefiner of it; whether or not he is ever given his just due, he should take satisfaction from the fact that he has written mystery novels of genuine distinction." – literary critic Richard Carpenter

Dan Fortune series, by Dennis Lynds, originally published under the pseudonym Michael Collins
Act of Fear, 1967
The Brass Rainbow, 1969
Night of the Toads, 1970
Walk a Black Wind, 1971
Shadow of a Tiger, 1972
The Silent Scream, 1973
Blue Death, 1975
The Blood-Red Dream, 1976
The Nightrunners, 1978
The Slasher, 1980
Freak, 1983
Minnesota Strip, 1987
Red Rosa, 1988
A Dangerous Job, 1989
Chasing Eights, 1990
The Irishman's Horse, 1991
Cassandra In Red, 1992

Paul Shaw series, by Dennis Lynds, originally published under the pseudonym Mark Sadler
The Falling Man, 1970
Here to Die, 1971
Mirror Image, 1972
Circle of Fire, 1973
Touch of Death, 1981
Deadly Innocents, 1986

Kane Jackson series, by Dennis Lynds, originally published under the pseudonym William Arden
A Dark Power, 1968
Deal in Violence, 1969
The Goliath Scheme, 1971

Die to a Distant Drum, 1972
Deadly Legacy, 1973

Buena Costa County series, by Dennis Lynds, originally published under the pseudonym John Crowe
Another Way to Die, 1972
A Touch of Darkness, 1972
Bloodwater, 1974
Crooked Shadows, 1975
When They Kill Your Wife, 1977
Close to Death, 1979

George Malcolm, private detective, by Dennis Lynds, originally published under the pseudonym Carl Dekker
Woman in Marble, 1973

Langford ("Ford") Morgan, ex-soldier, ex-CIA, ex-roustabout, by Dennis Lynds, originally published under the pseudonym Michael Collins
The Cadillac Cowboy, 1995

Other of his works include
science fiction novels, literary novels, mystery short stories, literary short stories, short story anthologies, and poetry.

Table of Contents

Chapter 1 1
Chapter 2 6
Chapter 3 11
Chapter 4 17
Chapter 5 24
Chapter 6 31
Chapter 7 37
Chapter 8 46
Chapter 9 50
Chapter 10 56
Chapter 11 62
Chapter 12 68
Chapter 13 73
Chapter 14 78
Chapter 15 84
Chapter 16 92
Chapter 17 98
Chapter 18 103
Chapter 19 109
Chapter 20 116
Chapter 21 122
Chapter 22 128
Chapter 23 135
Chapter 24 141
Chapter 25 149
Chapter 26 156

Chapter 27 163
Chapter 28 170

A Sneak Peek at the next Dan Fortune Mystery 174
Meet the Author: Dennis Lynds 179
The Back Cover 183

1

SAMMY WEISS once made seventeen passes in a row in a crap game where "two bits" meant twenty-five dollars, not a quarter. It was the event of his life, and they still tell the story around the Village and Lower East Side. It does not impress me. I was there.

But Sammy never forgot that once, briefly, he had been a big man. He was being the big man now where he sat in the only other chair in my one-room office.

"You swear I was with you twelve noon to two P.M.," Weiss said, "and it's a C-note for you."

He was expansive, come to buy the services of a poor detective, but his shadowed Levantine eyes did not look at me. Weiss is short, fat and soft, and his eyes never look at anyone. He wears a clean shirt, but his suits never fit. His floral ties sport a diamond stickpin that went out of style long ago. His overcoat is too long and has a fur collar. The fur shows bare hide where it has rubbed so long against his fat neck.

"Make it two hundred," he said. "I was with you, right?"

"You haven't had two hundred at one time in ten years," I said. "And I don't buy."

"Danny the Pirate, he's so honest?"

The old nickname showed how long Weiss has known me. A relic of the ancient career in juvenile thievery that had cost me my arm. Unrecorded history, I've got no police record. All I have is a missing arm and old acquaintances like Weiss.

"I lost my arm, not my brains. My mother didn't raise me to sell an alibi for two bills, and not in the dark."

"Your mother I could of bought for a dollar!"

I closed my eyes. A cold wind was blowing down the air-shaft and through my single window. A Siberian blast that made my stump ache. I opened my eyes. You can't really feel better by hitting a man weaker than you. At least, I never could. Maybe that's why I never made my mark in the world.

"Hell, Danny, I'm sorry," Weiss said.

He had begun to sweat. It was ten degrees outside, and not much higher in the office, but his face shined with sweat like a pale wet moon. Just as it had done years ago on his big night.

Weiss had begun with ten dollars, let the pot ride, and after his fifteenth straight pass there was $163,840 in that pot. Two more passes, maybe one, would have broken the game. That is the crapshooter's dream: to be the last man at a long table in an empty room, stacking his money.

I remember the stink of his sweat-soaked clothes as the gamblers waited. I can see his hands shaking as he reached to drag $160,000 from that pot, and hear him croaking, "Craps coming, I got the hunch. Crap this time for sure."

Crap had not come. He made two more passes before he crapped out, and when he walked out on stiff legs he left the game badly bent but not broken. The hard-faces smiled. They knew. Weiss walked out rich, but not a winner. He had won a battle; other men were going to win the war.

Now I said, gently for a born loser, "What trouble is it?"

"I don't know, Danny," he said, his hat held in both hands like a suppliant before a priest. "Freedman's after me."

He shuddered as if in pain. For Weiss, Detective Second Grade Bert Freedman was pain.

"You know," I said. "Tell it."

He looked at the ceiling as if trying to find some way of not knowing. "I went up to this guy in the Sixties: Jonathan Radford III. He got a nephew: Walter Radford IV. Like kings they got numbers." He tried to grin to make it all okay. "Anyway, Walter owes me $25,000 from a big poker game. I go to collect from the uncle, see? A girl opens the door and sends me to a kind of office. This Radford don't even turn around. He's by the open window, breathing! Silk robe! The big man. He lets me cool my heels a while. I say where's my money? He turns around, fast-like. He says no payoff! He says I can go whistle. He curses me out. So I throws a bluff at him, see? I say there'll be trouble, heads maybe get broken. He comes on me like he's nuts! He grabs me. He musses me up. I swing on him, maybe once. He goes over and just lies there. I mean, he don't get up. So I go to turn him over, when he starts groaning. I got scared. I beat it."

He stopped. I waited.

"That's all of it?" I said.

"What else? I mean, he went over, he was groaning, and I beat it," Weiss said. "Look, the doorman saw me go in, maybe one look. He wasn't there when I went out. One old lady in the lobby saw me going out fast, and that girl saw me when I went in. She didn't hardly look at me. How can they be sure? You tell Freedman I was with you, and it's us against Radford. A lot of guys look like me. He made a mistake."

It was so stupid, so full of holes, it was pitiful. An animal running blindly from a forest fire.

"Sammy," I said, "Radford knows your name."

"He don't!" Sammy said triumphantly. "I never told him."

"Then how do the police know?"

"I figure he give a description. Freedman hears that and comes after me first off."

"How do you know Freedman wants you?"

"I got friends. I made my window a jump ahead of the Cossack *golem* two hours ago. I shook him."

"Maybe it's something else."

"I ain't done nothing else. Gimme an alibi, Danny?"

"No. Go in. See what Freedman's got. Don't mention Radford until they do. If it is Radford, he started the fight."

"He's a blueblood, Danny, rich. Who listens to Sammy Weiss? They'll drop a year on me at least. I can't take it inside. All you got to do is alibi me. I know how it works. Our word against his. Only it's got to be two of us."

"No," I said. "It wouldn't help, and it'd hang me."

His moon face looked straight at me for almost the first time. "Okay, Dan, sure. Only go talk to the guy. Make him tell he started it. Talk to Freedman, you know? Tell him I got friends. Look, I ain't got two C-notes. I can get maybe fifty bucks."

"Freedman would laugh at me, and how do I prove this Radford hit first? What can I do, Sammy? Go in to the Lieutenant, skip Freedman. Tell your side of it straight."

He blinked at me. He got up. His lower lip quivered. He put on his hat and walked out. A small, fat man with a ragged fur collar and a diamond stickpin. A small man who walked small and who knew it.

For a year after the night that had been his triumph and his tragedy, Weiss had walked tall. He spent, or lost, that $160,000 in the year to prove how tall he was. All he proved was that he was not tall at all. His moment had come and he had failed it. Most men fail their big moment, but most can evade the knowledge of their failure. Weiss could not evade.

He had not crapped out on the sixteenth roll. He had rolled two more passes, and those two useless passes would haunt Weiss forever. They proved he did not have what it took. So he bluffs. His cow eyes tell the world that the next time he will let the pot ride all the way. He doesn't even fool himself. He knows he will always quit two passes too soon. Freedman probably wanted him for something about as important as rolling dice in public.

I hauled on my duffle coat and went out to eat.

On the dark street the wind blew a spray of old snow. I hunched inside my collar and headed for Eighth Avenue. As I neared the corner, I saw Weiss talking to a tallish, redheaded woman. She wore thick stage make-up, and black-net stage tights showed from under her fur coat. Her hair was almost orange and piled high. Weiss got into a taxi with her.

I went down to the Sevilla and had a *paella*. I thought about Marty, my woman. Marty was down in Philadelphia with a new show, so I thought about Sammy Weiss. I thought about his story, and a small point stuck out after a time and bothered me. If this Radford, or his nephew, owed Weiss $25,000, how could Sammy say that no one at Radford's apartment knew his name? It made no sense.

I finished my dinner and went over to Boyle's Tavern, where Joe Harris was working.

"You hear about Sammy Weiss winning $25,000?" I asked Joe.

"I ain't heard of him winning twenty-five cents," Joe said, and poured. Joe always slips me my first Irish free. "Where would Weiss get the stake to win that much, or the nerve to play for it anymore?"

"Yeh," I said.

I wondered what Weiss had really pulled, or tried to. I didn't wonder too hard. Not then.

2

I WOKE UP to pounding on my outside door. My watch read six-thirty. The dawn light was gray, and the temperature in my bedroom was like the arctic tundra.

I shivered out of bed and grabbed my robe. I turned on the oven and two of my gas heaters. With my income I can choose between one warm room or five cold ones. I like space, but it's a discouraging choice. While I lighted the heaters and wished I could afford five warm rooms without rearranging my psyche to fit the needs of the corporations, the pounding on my door did not let up.

I opened the door on Detective Bert Freedman. He was a short, stocky man with shoulders like a bear. He walked in without being invited, producing a warrant, or saying hello. It was a technical point I let pass. Freedman started a tour of my rooms.

I plugged in my coffeepot. Men who live alone too long, or live in too many places where no one knows them, develop habits instead of friends. A ready pot of coffee was my welcome to a new day. It was perking when Freedman faced me.

"You can tell me where Sammy Weiss is, or you can come down to the squad room."

"You can close the door behind you going out, or you can have some coffee."

"Don't get wise with me, Fortune!"

Freedman makes big fists for a short man. He's a hitter, a Johnny Broderick detective. But the famous Broderick was a good cop, hard and smart, while Freedman is a bad cop who is hard in place of being smart. The police have a normal quota of stupid men; no more and no less than any other big organization. I was no match for Freedman. I wouldn't have been with two hands, but I keep a hammer handy in my kitchen. In my work I need the police, but I draw the line at Freedman. I touched the hammer.

"I didn't ask you in," I said. "You've got no warrant, and I'm not a reasonable suspect in a felony. You're out of your precinct. Lay off, or I'll fight back and apologize later."

Freedman has no sense of humor. Vicious men seldom do. He watched me as if deciding whether I would really fight or not. His fists clenched and unclenched.

"Weiss told people he was going to hire you."

"He didn't," I said. "What's he wanted for?"

Freedman laughed. "He's one Jew-boy's gonna hang slow."

Freedman has a mission—to destroy any of his fellow Jews who break the law. A self-appointed scourge of the tribe.

"Why?" I said.

"He's dirt," Freedman said. "A bug, a grease spot. You see him, or hear from him, you tell me fast. Just me, no one else."

"If he'd shot Moses," I said, "I'd tell you last. I'd want him to get to the Tombs on his feet and breathing."

Freedman couldn't really hurt me as long as I was clean with Centre Street and my own precinct squad. He opened and closed his fists a few more times, and then he left. He slammed the door.

Outraged voices along the hall complained bitterly. I hardly heard them. My mind was on Sammy Weiss. Freedman had not acted as if he wanted Weiss for punching a man—not even a rich man.

The Medical Examiner's Building in New York is on the East Side near the river. It stands between the old buildings of Bellevue Hospital and the new buildings of New York University's Medical School. Snow had started falling again, and it hung over the river like a swirling mist as I went down into the main autopsy room.

I was looking for the night man, Mitch O'Dwyer. There was a covered body on one of the eight tables. A murdered man on a living room floor does not make me shiver the way a body on an autopsy table does. It's the impersonality of death that scares.

Mitch O'Dwyer looked up. "Trouble, Dan?"

"Do you have a Jonathan Radford III, Mitch?"

No matter how rich a man is, if he dies a violent death in New York he will end up on the autopsy table. In midtown that means in the M.E.'s morgue, and Mitch O'Dwyer makes the tags that go on the wrists of the dead.

"Yeh," Mitch said. "I remember that part about 'the third.'"

I wasn't really surprised, or I wouldn't have been there in the morgue.

"Can I see him, Mitch?"

"Make it fast. The docs'll be down soon."

There are 128 storage crypts in the morgue. New York is a big and violent city. The crypt Mitch opened contained a muscular man of medium size in his late fifties or so. He had been a handsome man with regular features, thick gray hair and an imperial beard, small eyes, and a thin, hard mouth. Weiss had been right. Radford looked rich and tough, like old Kaiser Wilhelm.

"Can I see the report, Mitch?"

"Is it important?"

"It could be."

"Okay, I'll look at it for you. Wait over in Phil's."

I went across the wide avenue to Phil's luncheonette. The snow was thick and blowing. I ordered two eggs and coffee. Mitch arrived before my second coffee. He sat down and read from a pad:

"Jonathan Ames Radford III; age 59; 146 East Sixty-third Street. Dead on arrival at his home of 17th Squad detectives called by George Foster Ames of the same address. Death was from a single knife wound in the left ventricle."

I sat up. "A knife, Mitch?"

"That was it. The wound was funny, some kind of knife with a wavy edge. It wasn't found."

"What about the time?"

"Cops got there at six-ten P.M. That was last night. The Doc estimated time of death between around noon to two-thirty P.M."

"Any other wounds or bruises?"

"No, and that's funny. In knifings they usually get bruises."

I paid Mitch his ten dollars and went back out into the wind on the avenue. (What Mitch does isn't legal, but he has six kids and the taxpayers hate to pay people they can't see working directly for their own benefit.)

In the driving snow I walked downtown toward the Lower East Side. I wanted to find Sammy Weiss. It could be that the police only wanted Weiss as a witness. That was not the way Freedman had acted, but you could never tell with a man like Freedman. Any chance to make Weiss sweat would be a pleasure for Freedman.

Sammy was not a violent man. He was, if anything, a soft man. On the other hand he hadn't seen anything like $25,000 in a long time, and if Radford had tried to welsh . . . ?

One way or the other it was murder, and, witness or suspect, Weiss's only play was to turn himself in. There's nowhere to run from murder.

He had come to me, and while I owed him nothing, everyone needs someone on their side. There are always gray areas, even in murder. It was possible that Weiss didn't even know that Radford was dead. Someone had to tell him, and better me than Freedman.

I plodded through the snow of the Village and the Lower East Side for the better part of the morning. I tried all Weiss's haunts I could remember: taverns, poolrooms, Turkish baths, horse rooms, and the dingy cafeterias where lone men like Sammy eat. Freedman had been most places before me. No one had seen Weiss since 3:00 A.M. last night. That made me wonder.

No one sticks to the old places like a solitary gambler down on his luck, except a sailor. To a sailor the ship is home, mother and family. To a piece of flotsam like Weiss, home is his haunts.

As a last resort I checked his room on St. Marks Place. I did not expect him to be there. He wasn't. I stopped for a beer.

Sammy was on the run or hiding. Without money he could not run far, and he could not get money because the police would know everywhere he could hope to get it. Without money he could not hide long, either. So he had more money than I had suspected, or someone was hiding him. It let me out. If he had stabbed Radford, only a lawyer could really help him. If he hadn't stabbed anyone, he didn't seem to need my volunteer aid.

I went home and cooked a can of soup to warm me. I watched the snow outside the window. The tall buildings uptown were vague ghosts through the swirling flakes. I thought about Marty. I thought about going down to Philly to see her. But I would only be in her way. A girl trying to make it in her first real show doesn't want a steady lover hanging around to scare off people.

I got my coat. I couldn't spend the day thinking about what Marty was doing in Philadelphia. At least I could find out how bad it was for Weiss. Not from the police. They would only figure I was in touch with Weiss and sweat me. I would investigate. At least keep busy.

Maybe I was just curious. Being a detective gets to be a habit, and a murder is like a mountain—it's there.

3

THE APARTMENT HOUSE on East Sixty-third Street where Jonathan Radford had lived was a massive, gingerbread gray building built in the twenties for the true rich. Its upper stories were lost in the heavy snow.

"Radford apartment," I said to the doorman.

He was obviously under orders to keep the murder quiet. A foursome looking for a taxi appeared in the lobby. He didn't even ask who I was.

"Apartment 17, left elevator, rear."

It was a small, self-service elevator that served only two apartments on each floor. It delivered me to a tiny foyer for apartment 17. I rang.

The man who answered the door was tall, gray-haired, and looked something like the body in the morgue without the beard. He had a large nose, the pink face a man gets when he is habitually shaved by barbers, and a wrinkled neck he tried to hide by holding his head too high. I had a mental flash—I knew his face. How?

"Mr. Ames?" I guessed.

"Yes, I . . . What do you want? I'm very busy."

He passed his hand over his face. He seemed nervous, out of focus. His suit had wide lapels and an old-fashioned cut, but looked custom-made within the year. The cuffs of his shirt came four inches out of his sleeves and were linked with rubies. The cuffs, and his high collar, were starched stiff.

"I'm a detective, Mr. Ames," I said, not mentioning that I was private, or giving my name. Why ask for trouble from the police? "I'd like to ask some questions about the murder."

He nodded vaguely. "The murder, yes. I . . . I really can't believe he's gone. Jonathan. Dead! That stupid animal!"

"Can I come in?" I said.

"What? Oh, yes, of course. I don't see what . . ."

He trailed off. I walked into a living room as large as four of my rooms—an elegant, high-ceilinged room that had been lived in for a long and comfortable time. The furniture glowed. Most of it was from one of the French periods, but there were enough odd pieces to show that no hired decorator had laid it out.

"Now, if you'll . . ." I began, trying to sound official.

Ames was staring at me. He was looking at my empty sleeve. Suspicion flickered in his eyes.

"I was under the impression that the murderer of my cousin was being pursued. The Weiss person. A matter of time."

"The police say Weiss killed him?"

"Of course! Who else . . . You did say you were a detective?"

"Private," I admitted.

"Private? You mean for hire?" He was all alert now. "Is there some factor involved that I am not aware of?"

"I'm not allowed to discuss my client, Mr. Ames," I said, which was more or less true—if I had had a client. "Perhaps you could tell me about yesterday?"

It is amazing how much the rich, the secure, accept without bothering to question. They're not used to being deceived, and they aren't afraid of much. What can hurt them? Ames didn't even ask for my credentials. All he did was show annoyance. He seemed confused by the whole affair, and I was a flea under his collar.

"What? Oh, yes, yes. What do you want?"

"Was your cousin expecting any visitors besides Weiss?"

"He wasn't expecting anyone. He had a slight cold or he would have been at his office as usual."

"So he made the appointment with Weiss yesterday morning?"

"I don't know when he made it. I didn't see him after breakfast. When Walter and I left, Jonathan was out."

"Walter Radford lives here?"

"No, no," Ames said testily. "Walter has his own apartment. I presume he came to talk to Jonathan. After Jonathan went out, Walter came back to my rooms and suggested we share a taxi as far as my club. He knows I always lunch at the club if I'm not working in a show."

Then I knew where I had seen him before. "I've seen you on television, haven't I? Broadway, too. I saw you play a high commissioner of a British colony. You were good."

"Why, thank you." He beamed now. "It's gratifying to be recognized, although it says more for your sharp eyes than my fame. I'm not exactly in demand. TV bits, mostly. An actor has to work."

"Rich men don't often go in for acting."

"The one thing in my life I am really proud of, Mr. . . . What did you say your name was?"

He had me. If you want to stay anonymous, don't praise a man. People always want to know who is flattering them.

"Fortune," I said. "Dan Fortune."

"My pride, Mr. Fortune, is that I tried to carve my own place in a hard arena. Most of our family tend to regal indolence. Not that I'm rich. Through devious twists of family history, Jonathan and his brother, Walter Senior, were the rich ones. The rest of us are not impoverished, but we are not rich. I shared this apartment with Jonathan for twenty-five years, but he owned it."

I took the opportunity of his better humor. "Can you tell me anything more, Mr. Ames? For instance, what led the police to Weiss?"

"I found his name on Jonathan's desk calendar."

"Careless of him to leave his name."

"I presume he isn't a mental giant. Besides, it seems clear that he struck, probably, in anger. I suppose he panicked."

It was a pretty good description of Weiss, and of the only way he might have killed a man.

"You didn't see Jonathan again after the morning?"

"No. I came home at half-past five. When he did not appear for our cocktails at six, I went to his study. I found him on the floor in a pool of dried blood. I'm afraid I was sick. I had a drink. Then I called the police."

"Where did he go that morning? When did he get back?"

"We learned later that he had been to lunch with Deirdre. She says they returned here at about one o'clock."

"Who's Deirdre?"

"Deirdre Fallon, young Walter's lady friend. She actually let Weiss into the apartment before she left."

"What time was that?"

"She says about one-fifteen. When Gertrude, Walter's mother, came to call at about two o'clock, she got no answer."

I made a mental timetable. Radford had been alive at one-fifteen when Weiss came. Say fifteen minutes or so for Sammy in the study: one-thirty. At two o'clock no one answered the door. I wasn't sure I wanted to find Weiss. Not if they were all telling the truth.

"What about enemies? Business troubles? Who gets rich now?"

But I had lost him. He might have been shaken by the murder, and I had flattered him for a moment, but he was not a fool. His eyes had hardened while I was thinking over the timetable.

"Are you working for this Weiss, Mr. Fortune?"

"In a way," I admitted.

His voice was flint. "I see. You believe him innocent?"

"I want to hear a real motive."

"Isn't $25,000 enough for a man like that?"

"You mean the money Walter owed him? Why would he . . . ?"

"I mean the $25,000 he stole, Mr. Fortune."

So there it was. If I were the police, I would be after Weiss.

"The money was taken from the apartment?" I said.

"From a drawer in the study," Ames said. "Weiss was here to collect the money, Mr. Fortune. He was here at the time of the murder. The weapon was at hand. The money is gone."

I said nothing. What could I say?

"Now you come to ask questions while Weiss is apparently still at large," Ames said. "When a rich man is murdered, only a fool fails to consider anyone who might gain by his murder. I've thought about it all night. There is no one. You can believe me when I tell you there was no one with a good enough reason to murder Jonathan. There is only your Weiss."

I nodded. "Can I look at the study?"

"I believe I . . ." he began angrily, and stopped. He hesitated. "Very well. I don't see why not."

The study was down a small corridor. It was book-lined and leather-furnished. A stain on a large rug showed that the body had been partly behind the desk. There were four windows. They were all closed and inaccessible from outside except to a bird. The room had one door, and it had been thoroughly searched.

I went out and stood in the small corridor. To the right it led into the kitchen. There was a back door to the kitchen. It was locked inside by a spring lock. Through it was the usual back staircase for garbage, deliveries and fire. The lock did not seem to have been tampered with.

I returned to the living room and thanked Ames. He nodded. His well-tended face was frosty. I was nosing, unasked, into his affairs. There's nothing like self-interest to bring a man out of shock or sorrow.

In the lobby I braced the doorman. "What time did Radford come home yesterday afternoon?"

"Around one o'clock, with the Fallon girl. I already told the Captain. I seen the fat guy go up maybe one-fifteen. Miss Fallon come down right after that, like I said."

He was eying my missing arm. He assumed I was a cop, and the arm probably made me look like a tough cop.

"When did the fat guy come down?"

"I didn't see. I had to help old lady Gadsden with her groceries. Two million bucks, and she carries her own stuff."

"Where do the back stairs open out?"

"Alley in the rear. It locks inside, only you know."

I knew. Half the time it would be open. I went out into the snow. It was still coming down, but not as heavy. I started up to the corner, thinking about what I could do next. George Ames had sounded pretty certain about no one else killing Radford. He could be right—as far as he knew. But there was another side to the coin, a side Ames might not know.

Maybe Sammy Weiss had killed and stolen $25,000, but he hadn't acted last night like a man with $25,000. He had been really scared, I knew that much, and it wasn't like him not to flash that money at me if he wanted help. On top of that, how did Weiss get owed $25,000 in the first place?

At the corner I decided to look closer into what Sammy had been doing lately. I started crosstown for the subway. I got two steps.

A car pulled up beside me and two men got out—one from each side of the car.

4

I DIDN'T TRY to run. There was no point. They had me boxed, and I waited in the snow for them to come up to me. They came on both sides, wary.

Then I saw the buggy-whip aerial on the car, and I saw the way they walked. Not exactly with arrogance, but with the cool assurance that comes from the massive power of law, right, and privilege that rests on them—cops.

"Fortune?" one of them said when he reached me.

"Would it help to say no?"

"Are you Daniel Fortune?" the second one asked without a smile.

"I'm Daniel Fortune," I said. "Who are you?"

"Come on," the first one said.

They conducted me to the car. I didn't know either of them, which probably meant they were from the local precinct. The man in the back of the car wasn't from the local precinct, and I knew him: Captain Gazzo from Homicide down at Centre Street.

"Hello, Dan," Gazzo said.

"Captain," I said.

I've known Gazzo all my life, since the days when he was a young cop and a friend of my mother's after my father faded out, but he's "Captain" when there are other cops around. It's a big city, New York, and Gazzo is the law. He was the law now. He didn't ask me to get in the car with him. I leaned in at the rear window, snow melting on my neck. That seemed to be where he wanted me. Interrogation is an art.

"Where's Sammy Weiss, Dan?"

"I don't know. I saw him early last night, not since."

"He hired you to work for him?"

"No."

"What did he tell you last night?"

"That he hit a man named Jonathan Radford. That Freedman was after him, and that he's scared of Freedman."

"Hit?" Gazzo said.

"That's what he told me."

Gazzo seemed to be trying to decide just how stupid I was this time. While I waited for him to decide, I thought about George Ames. It was obvious now that Ames had let me look at the study so he could make a call to the police and report me.

Gazzo decided. "George Ames called Chief of Detectives McGuire, Dan. He doesn't like you around. McGuire called me. I was up here on the case, so I came around to give you the word."

"Ames goes high," I said.

"Men like George Ames call a chief of detectives the way you and I call a messenger. He wouldn't even think about anyone lower. He knows McGuire personally, Dan. You have any real reason for thinking Weiss isn't guilty? Any facts?"

"No," I admitted. My neck was getting very wet.

Gazzo didn't care about my neck. "Radford was an important man. There's a stink already—hoodlums running loose; crime in the streets; no one safe in his home: the usual. We want Weiss."

"It wasn't a random crime, Captain. Weiss was invited in."

Gazzo ignored me. "Facts, and experience, tell us that Weiss made the mistake he's been ready to make all his life. Everything points to it, nothing points away from it. You have nothing, Dan. You don't even have a legitimate client. Up top they don't want you muddying the waters and maybe helping Weiss without meaning to."

"Maybe the waters need muddying."

"You want me to tell the Chief that?"

I leaned in the window. "Look, Captain, I haven't been nosing around long enough to even have a hunch. Weiss came to me, and I've been sort of automatically following up. Maybe it's reflex, or maybe it's a subconscious feeling that Sammy needs help from someone, but I want to find out more."

"You're saying we won't find out all there is to know?"

I took a deep breath. "I'm not sure you'll try. When you have a prime suspect, you don't go around fishing for new suspects in the shadows. No police force could, Gazzo. Until you rule out Weiss, you won't look for anyone else."

"You're saying we won't find out if he's innocent?"

"I'm saying you won't think about anyone else while you have Weiss. You've got too much crime and too few men. You can miss things. Remember that kid in Brooklyn who sat in jail for ten months with everything pointing to him until one of your men, on a hunch and his own time, proved the kid was innocent? Maybe no one will get a hunch about Weiss. Maybe you'll take too long, and facts will disappear. Maybe Weiss is so scared he'll panic and get gunned down. Even if he's guilty, Captain, I might turn up some mitigating circumstances."

Gazzo just sat there. "The Chief doesn't want you in this, Dan. I told him you've got a good record, so he won't make it official, but stay out of our way, and co-operate. Plain enough?"

"I'll do the best I can."

He didn't push the message any farther. He signaled the driver, and the car pulled away, leaving me alone in the snow. I felt very alone. The power of the police over me, like most power in our society, was mainly economic. But I have an edge. I don't have to be a detective or work in New York. No one depends on my success. I have no status to keep and no investment to tie me down. I had to give up a lot of comforts and trinkets to get that edge. In a money society you can be independent with money, or independent of money. Anywhere in between you're under the thumb.

That is true enough, but I didn't kid myself. The police have other powers not so legitimate. A private detective can bend a lot of laws, and a chief of detectives can turn a bend into a break. That power is harder to use in a city the size of New York, but it was there. I would have to be careful.

I would have liked to ask Gazzo about what he knew, about why the police were so sure Weiss was their man, about the circumstances and the alibis of others, but you don't ask those things when you're being told that the higher powers don't want you around. I would have to dig myself—especially into that $25,000 Weiss said he had won from Walter Radford.

Cellars Johnson sat alone at the green table in the cellar on Houston Street where he holds his steady game. He was dealing poker hands to himself.

"Take a hand," Cellars said.

Cellars squeezed his cards as if it were 4:00 A.M. in his regular game and all the night's winnings were in the pot. His black face sweated, but his eyes were a blank wall. In a real game even his sweat glands would have been under control, and there is nothing that happens around the Village that Cellars doesn't know.

"Have you seen Sammy Weiss?" I asked.

Cellars studied his cards. I had jacks over fives.

"Bet fifty," Cellars said. "I saw him maybe two A.M. last night."

"Raise fifty," I said. It's easy to gamble big in the mind, for fun. "Did he play last night?"

"He couldn't show the cash."

"How much cash do you ask now?"

"A hundred to sit down," Cellars said. "Gimme two cards."

I took one card myself. I still had jacks and fives.

"Bet the pot," Cellars said.

"Raise the pot," I said. The big plunger. "I heard Weiss won $25,000 from a kid named Walter Radford."

Cellars didn't seem to hear me. He tossed in his cards. "Let's see what you raised a pot bet on."

I showed him my two pair. It was just a game for laughs. Cellars didn't laugh.

"You don't even see a pot bet by a two-card draw with a lousy two pair," Cellars instructed. "I folded three queens."

He was telling me that in a real game I might get away with that kind of playing once, maybe twice, but in the end I'd be begging cab fare. Cellars can't play bad poker even for fun.

I said, "You know anything about this Walter Radford?"

Cellars gathered the cards. "You for or against Weiss?"

"For, I think."

He began to shuffle. He needs the cards in his hands. "A party named Radford had Costa's place up in North Chester closed down ten months ago."

"Who's Costa?"

"Carmine Costa. Independent operator. No book or numbers. A casino operation with some private games."

"Why was he closed?"

"Who knows? You know Westchester, Dan. Costa opened up in the next town." Cellars began to deal solitaire. "Weiss ain't such a bad guy. I hear the heat's on him big. Freedman been around twice." He looked up at me. "Paul Baron, too."

"Paul Baron?" I said. The name rang a faint bell, but I couldn't place it.

"Alias The Baron, Baron Paul Ragotzy, some other names," Cellars said. "A con artist; the badger games. He handles the cards, too."

"He was looking for Weiss?"

"Once last night, and once today."

"What did he want?"

"Just Weiss."

"How about a woman? A redhead, tall, probably a showgirl or stripper in some club."

Cellars shook his head. "No, just Freedman and Baron. Only one of Baron's women is a tall redhead. Misty Dawn. She works the Fifth Street Club."

I stood up. "Thanks, Cellars."

Cellars nodded, but he was thinking. I waited. He seemed to be making some decision.

"Weiss ain't such a bad guy," Cellars said again.

I still waited. I knew that Cellars was deciding to tell me something. It was a hard decision for him.

"There was a game, about two months ago," Cellars said. "I played. Baron was there. He brought a kid. Walter Radford IV. I remember that number part, you know?"

"Thanks again," I said.

"Sure," Cellars said. "Come back for the action."

The snow had stopped, and the Fifth Street Club was open. I went down into the dim light of the deserted bar and ordered an Irish. It was just too early for the cocktail hour. In the main room one drunken group was trying to eat what had to be a very late lunch. The bartender had cunning eyes and a loose mouth.

"I'd like to buy Misty Dawn a drink," I said.

"So would a lot of guys."

I laid a five-dollar bill beside my whisky. In a club like that one, the girls usually had orders to drink with any customer, but it was early. The five was to make the bartender eager to help me. He took the bill and vanished toward the small stage. In the main room the waiters leaned on the walls and yawned.

The bartender returned. He nodded. A minute or so later I sensed someone come out of the curtained doorway at stage left. She slid onto the stool beside me in a dead heat with a whisky sour from the bartender.

"Hello," she said.

Her voice was deep and rough from shouting songs into noisy rooms. She wore her full work make-up, with mounds of orange-red hair piled on her head. Her body was trim and inviting in a black velvet leotard and net tights.

She smiled at me. "I'm Misty Dawn, Mr. . . . ?"

"Fortune," I said. "I'm looking for Sammy Weiss."

She stood up. "Get lost."

"I want to help Sammy."

Her eyes were black in the dim light. They might have been brown, or green, or gray if I could have seen them.

"I don't know Sammy Weiss," she said.

"How about a Radford? Jonathan or Walter."

"How about the Mayor?" she said. "What are you, mister?"

"A friend of Sammy Weiss," I said. "How about Paul Baron? He wants Weiss, too."

"Okay, I know Paul Baron. That's one out of four."

"Do you know what Baron wants with Weiss?"

"I don't even know if Paul knows the guy."

"Yes you do," I said. "I saw you with Weiss on Eighth Avenue last night."

"No you didn't," she said, and walked away.

I watched her go. She walked nicely in that leotard. I watched until she went through the door backstage. Then I paid and left.

5

THERE WERE PLENTY of Radfords in the telephone book, and enough Walter Radfords, but only one Walter Radford IV. Those numerals seemed to mean a lot to the Radfords. The address was Gramercy Park.

I was in Mary's Italian Restaurant just off Seventh Avenue when I looked up Walter Radford, and I stopped for some *shrimp marinara*. When I went out into the street again to find a taxi, it was dark and quiet and ten degrees colder since the snow had stopped.

The taxi dropped me in front of a new and shiny building, all glass and red brick, that was not exactly on Gramercy Park although it had the address. The lobby was elegant but small, and there was no doorman. Walter Radford IV had apartment 12. I rode the stainless steel elevator to the third floor.

There was no answer to my ringing. I looked up and down the empty corridor. The door had an ordinary spring lock, with enough gap between door and frame. I took out the stiff plastic rectangle I carry, slipped it between door and frame and against the lock, and pressed hard. I worked the rectangle. The lock gave with a click and I skinned a knuckle.

Inside I switched on the light. The risk was worth not being taken for a burglar. It was a gaudy apartment of chrome, plastic and bad modern—designed without art and selected without taste. The main room was a mess, as if it was lived in by someone who was rebelling against his mother who had made him pick up his toys and dirty clothes when he was a boy. A poker table was strewn with cards, and a toy roulette wheel on the couch was surrounded by loose chips.

I went to work looking through the chests, bookcases, table drawers, and the one desk. For what? Something to connect Walter Radford to Paul Baron or anyone else except Weiss. I didn't find much: books about gambling; decks of cards; Playbills; dirty paper napkins with figures scrawled on them; letters that proved that the Radford-Ames family was large and that Walter had a lot of friends. From the way the letters read, the friends were from prep school and college and hadn't changed much.

There was a small, 7-mm. Belgian automatic in a drawer. It was loaded. There was a large address book filled, mostly, with the names of men and gilt-edged business outfits. Paul Baron's name did not appear in the address book or anywhere else. I became hypnotized by the slow reading. The sound of the elevator jerked me out of it.

I jumped to the light switch. Maybe it was someone for another apartment. It wasn't. The footsteps stopped outside the door. I slid into the bedroom, behind the door.

The outside door opened. The lights went on. A long pause.

"Walter? Are you here, Walter?"

A woman's voice, low. I waited. She moved and a drawer opened. I heard her pick up the telephone. I pressed against the door to try to hear. I didn't have to try. She spoke loud and clear:

"I have a pistol. I am calling the police. You left marks on the rug. If you have no reason to be here, come out with both hands in front of you. If I don't see your hands, I shoot."

Her voice was quiet, cultured and steady—a finishing-school voice. She didn't sound scared. I was. There are a lot of dangers for a one-armed man. This was one of them.

I said, loud, "I have only one hand. I'll come out of the bedroom with my right hand out, my left shoulder forward."

I stepped out—nervous. I showed my left side.

"Sit down," she said, looking at my stump. "On the couch."

I sat.

"Who are you? Who let you in? Walter?"

She had the Belgian automatic in her right hand, the telephone in her left. A young woman with a fine, classic oval face and no make-up. Chestnut hair hung long on her shoulders. Tallish, she had good legs. She probably had good hips and breasts, but the severe blue suit she wore did not display her hips, and in the suit she had nothing as obvious as breasts; she had a bosom.

The way she used Walter Radford's first name, the fact that she had a key, and the way she looked at my empty sleeve told me who she had to be. George Ames must have described my arm.

"No, Miss Fallon," I said. "I'm afraid I came snooping."

"You're the private detective Uncle George reported?"

"Dan Fortune," I acknowledged.

"Show me," she said, "and open your coat."

"I don't carry a gun," I said, but I carefully opened both sides of my coat. Then I fished out my wallet and tossed my license to her.

She picked it up and looked at it. She did not put down the automatic, but she had put down the telephone. I felt a little better. I hadn't wanted to face Gazzo again.

"Uncle George said the police were going to stop you."

"I guess I talk faster than Ames," I said. "The police can make mistakes, Miss Fallon, and they really want the truth."

"They aren't convinced that this Weiss creature killed Uncle Jonathan?"

"They're convinced, but they're willing to let me waste my time—grudgingly."

She nodded slowly, thinking. She put the gun down on the telephone table, sat down, and lighted a cigarette.

"So you came here to investigate Walter?"

The word for Deirdre Fallon was "poised." That was something of a surprise, since she didn't look a day over twenty. The second word was "class." Neat, graceful class. The third word I had in mind was "virginal," but there was something about the way she handled her body that held me back on that word.

"I came to talk to Walter," I said. "He wasn't here. I decided to nose around. I'd still like to talk to Walter."

"Walter is in North Chester at his mother's. At least I supposed he was. When I saw those marks on the rug . . ."

"It was possible he was here," I said. "He could have let me in. That was lucky for me. Now maybe I could talk to you?"

"To me?"

"You had lunch with Jonathan Radford. Where?"

"The Charles XII on Lexington Avenue."

"How was he? His mood?"

"Normal, I'd say. Perhaps a little testy."

"As if he had something on his mind?"

"I suppose so. I didn't notice at the time. We talked about Walter and myself."

"Did anything happen? Anything unusual?"

"No. We talked, ate, and went home. Walter wasn't at the apartment, so I left. As I was leaving, this fat man in an awful old overcoat rang the bell and asked for Jonathan. I sent him into the study and left."

"Did you know Walter owed $25,000?"

"Yes. Walter gambles and usually loses. It's happened before." There was a kind of weariness in her voice.

"You don't gamble with him?"

"Why do you say that?"

"Because you apparently didn't know Weiss. Or did you?"

"No, I didn't know him. I don't know him."

"So if Walter owed the $25,000 to Weiss, he must have lost the money without you around."

She stabbed her cigarette out in an ashtray, stood, and walked to the picture window of the room. The window gave a fine view of shadowy tenements. I had a better view—her lean, but curved figure against the night sky. She stood there, lighted another cigarette, then turned and went back to her chair.

"Weiss was only a messenger. Sent to try to collect," she said. "Walter owed the money to a man named Paul Baron. It happened over a period of time."

"You know Paul Baron?"

"I know Mr. Baron. A smooth animal. Walter told him that Jonathan wouldn't pay this time. He told Baron that he would pay the debt off in installments. It seems that Baron had other ideas."

"Do the police know that the money was owed to Baron?"

"No. Walter is afraid of Baron. He sees no reason to involve Baron. Weiss came to Jonathan, not Baron."

"It was Baron's $25,000," I said.

"You think we should tell the police?"

"I know you should."

"Yes, all right, but I'd rather Walter told them."

"As long as someone does," I said. "Where did you go after you left Jonathan with Weiss?"

"To my hairdresser. I had a one-thirty appointment. I was there until three-thirty. Is that what you want to know?"

"Yes," I said. "Where was Walter all this time? He and Ames say they left the apartment before noon, right?"

"He took the twelve-ten train from Grand Central for North Chester. He was there all afternoon. He was there when Jonathan was . . . found." Her voice rose in pitch, the words coming out faster. "Uncle George was at his club. Mrs. Radford was there, but could not get in. I don't know where three hundred cousins were! The butler was in North Chester!"

She stopped on a high, rising note; breathless. Her chaste bosom heaved. She drew deeply on her cigarette. "Leave us alone, Mr. Fortune. This has been a horrible shock to the family. Such a stupid death for a man like Jonathan. Go away with your dirty questions. Can't you understand how terrible it is for the family?"

"It's pretty terrible for Sammy Weiss."

"He killed a man! For money!"

"Maybe," I said.

"No one else was there! Don't you think the police have checked?"
"How about Paul Baron?"
"Then talk to Baron!"
"Do you know where I could find him?"
"No! I mean, I've met him at quite a few places. At this hour . . ." She chewed at her lip. "There's an apartment on University Place where I've met him about this time." She gave me the address.

I stood up. "I'd still like to talk to Walter."

"I'll tell him."

She had recovered her cool exterior. On my way out I picked her blue cloth coat from the floor inside the door. I handed it to her. When she took it, our hands touched. I felt the touch low in my back where you feel a woman who has something you suddenly know you could want very much. I sensed that she felt it, too. She stiffened, and her nostrils flared quickly. I smiled. She backed off, her eyes dark and hostile. I left.

University Place wasn't far, so I walked. It was cold, and still, and the crust of frozen snow crunched under my feet on the dark streets. I thought about Sammy Weiss who just automatically played the big man, who had to say it had been his own $25,000 he had gone to collect. I had a sinking feeling that Weiss was not only running from a murder charge, he was running with $25,000 Paul Baron considered belonged to him.

The University Place building was big and bright with lights. I went up to the apartment Deirdre Fallon had named. I got no answer to my ringing. This lock was a deadfall, police-type. I couldn't open it if I had wanted to. I rang some more. When there was still no answer, I went back down and across to the I.R.T.

On the uptown platform I walked to the rear away from the thickest part of the early night crowd. I figured I'd have a new try at George Ames. He'd called the cops to get me off the case awful fast. If that didn't work, I could try to find Weiss again. I thought some more about Weiss running with the police after him and with Baron after him. Baron could be the worse danger.

I was in the air and falling!

Out over the subway tracks, clawing air.

I braced to hit the tracks, and heard the train coming.

Then time seemed to stop, reverse, blend past and present and future all together in the same instant.

I heard the train and felt the push at the same time.

I saw, in a brief flash, a slender man in pale gray. A handsome face turned for one intent look at me. A trim gray back walking away. A gray Homburg—jaunty. I thought: He's killed me.

I fell, and saw the gray man, and heard the train, and knew I was dead, and saw a train roar past me all in the same moment.

I hit the tracks and knew with great clarity that I was not dead because Astor Place was a local station. You see, on the I.R.T. the local and express often come almost side by side. I had been pushed by the sound, not the sight, of the train. The express was some six cars ahead of the local. A mistake, you see? He had pushed me six cars too soon.

I lay in between the tracks, and the local came and stopped above me. I lay in an icy stream of water. Voices: Hey! Hey! You okay? Yes, yes! I'm okay! In time they would move the train. I would get up, wipe myself, go on.

I rolled from under and walked across the express tracks to the downtown platform. I climbed up. They stared. Subway cops yelled. A train came and I got on. I rode down four stops. I thought. I got off and went up into the night. I found a taxi. I went to Pennsylvania Station. There was a train for Philadelphia. Marty, that was what I wanted.

I sat and watched the Jersey Flats, the factories, the towns, the pine woods around Princeton. I shook. I saw Marty's face in the dark window. She would wipe off the dirt and kiss me. I rode all the way to Trenton before I remembered that Marty had her own needs. I got off and waited two hours for the train back.

When I got home I locked my door and sat at a window and drank Irish whisky. I watched the night sky. When I went to bed, I began to shake again. I shivered without control until I fell asleep.

6

LIFE BEGINS in darkness and ends in darkness and in between is a nightmare.

A man in a bar in Algiers told me that. It was in my mind when I woke up to the gray cold of another day.

All you can do, that man said, is stay out of it. He may be right, but life is short. If you stay out you'll never know if you could have done something to make it less a nightmare. Like doing something about men who push other men under trains.

I was angry, and lay in bed enjoying the anger that had replaced the shaking of last night. I also thought about our ability to forget once an immediate threat has passed. It's our strength, I suppose, but also our weakness, and in the safe light of day I was sure no one could kill me. Stupid, of course, but without that belief, who could go ahead being a detective or anything else?

After a big breakfast to prove how good my nerves were, I spent the morning looking for Weiss again. I walked with one eye looking behind. I was brave, but not crazy. I didn't find a smell of Weiss, but I found that Paul Baron was still looking.

In the afternoon I checked out Deirdre Fallon. She was a regular at the Charles XII, she was well known, and she had been there with Radford. Her hairdresser backed her up, too. George Ames also checked out, but not as definitely. He had arrived at his club around noon all right, and had left around 5:00 P.M., but it was a big club with many doors, and Ames had not been with someone all the time.

I took the late afternoon train for North Chester. When I got off, there was a clean tang to the cold air: country air. The suburban town had a rural feel, with tree-lined streets, and a single old black limousine at the taxi stand. When we were out of the town and in the country, I asked the driver if he had seen Walter Radford get off the train on Monday.

"Come in on the one-fourteen. That's the twelve-ten out of the city. He took my cab. Old lady Radford come in on the three-two; the two-eight out of the city. Cops already asked me that. You a cop?"

"Private," I said.

"You don't say?"

The driver glanced at my empty sleeve and looked like he would like to talk some more, but I wasn't in the mood to tell any of my stories about losing the arm. We finally turned through a high iron gate and went along a curving drive through thick woods deep in snow to a house set in a large, snow-covered lawn.

It was a big house, but austere. The simple three-story brick center section was over a hundred and fifty years old. Two white frame wings had been added later, but no later than 1850. My driver had another train to meet, but he'd come back in an hour unless I called earlier. I knocked and waited in the brittle cold and impossible silence of a country twilight.

A short, dark man in a butler's outfit answered the door. Walter Radford was not at home. I gave my name and asked if I could talk to Mrs. Radford. The butler bowed me into an elegant entry hall and vanished through sliding doors to the left. A fine Federal Period staircase curved upward at the rear of the entry hall. A thin woman came through the sliding doors.

"Mr. Fortune? I'm Gertrude Radford."

She had the neat white hair, veined hands, and loose skin of her years, but there was a youthfulness about her. It was her eyes: wide, blue, almost innocent eyes. They were the eyes of someone who had faced few hard knocks, and who had never had to doubt anything. She wore a long black silk dress. Her pale face and nervous hands were the only signs that she might be disturbed by what had happened.

"I'd like to talk about Monday, Mrs. Radford? About your brother-in-law?"

"You're the detective George and Deirdre mentioned," she said. "I don't understand what you want. The police assure us that the man will be caught soon. He must be put away."

"They'll throw away the key."

"Don't be sarcastic, Mr. Fortune," she snapped, and frowned. "We are at coffee. You'll join us for a cup."

It was a command. I followed her into a dining hall of ornate sideboards, high-backed chairs, and a center table as long as six pool tables. Portraits of grim men from the past hung on the walls, all of them having a vague resemblance to the late Jonathan Radford and to George Ames. There were some fifteen people in the room. One of them was George Ames. They were all drinking coffee.

"How do you like it prepared, Mr. Fortune?" Gertrude Radford said.

The question would have been a surprise except that I was looking at the sideboards. There were percolators of every type; drip pots; filter-paper pots; silex types; espresso pots; one large urn; pots for boiling; and some ways of making coffee I couldn't even name.

"We each brew our own, Mr. Fortune, in our own way," Mrs. Radford said. "A family tradition going back over a hundred years. Coffee was the original Radford-Ames business. I myself favor a simple percolator."

"Percolator is fine," I said.

She led me into a corner. For a time we sat and drank. Coffee was sacred. It was good coffee. I watched the whole crew mothering their pots and cups, and all at once it gave me a chill. It was like a blood ritual with the celebrants drinking the blood of their ancestors at the high altar of family. A tribal rite designed, as all rites are designed, to keep the members inside and everyone else outside.

Mrs. Radford brought me out of my visions. "You're suggesting, Mr. Fortune, that there is doubt about what happened to Jonathan?"

"I don't know what happened to Jonathan," I said.

"The police seem sure this Weiss . . ."

"Sure isn't the same as knowing," I said.

A man's voice answered me: "That is a cynical statement, Mr. Fortune, and stubborn. You're more competent than you look."

George Ames stood over me. He wore evening clothes now—white tie and tails. He looked good.

"The police talked to me," I said. "They'll let me hang myself. Maybe we could talk about Jonathan's enemies now?"

"Influence didn't get rid of you, perhaps answers will," Ames said. He took a black cigarette case from his inner pocket and selected an elegant cigarette with gold trim. "Every man makes enemies in sixty years, but there was no one recent or special. Murder is drastic, Fortune. It takes a powerful reason, don't you think? There was no enemy of that magnitude."

"Business?"

Ames smoked, smiled. "Jonathan was chairman of Radford Industries. It's actually a financial holding company: impersonal, collective, almost anonymous. Jonathan's death will change nothing for anyone."

"Who gets the business now? Who gets his money?"

Mrs. Radford answered that. "Jonathan's personal money goes all over the family. He made no secret of that. He was a bachelor, and at least fifty people will share in his will."

"His real wealth," Ames added, "was his holdings in Radford Industries. Everyone in the family has some shares. I have a few thousand myself, but Jonathan held fifteen percent. That chunk gives control of the company; he would never break it up. I assume it will go intact to Walter as the only young Radford."

"It will," Mrs. Radford said, "together with the five percent my husband had and Jonathan controlled since my husband died."

"So Walter gets the business?" I said.

Ames laughed. It was a loud laugh. Almost too loud. "The stock doesn't mean the power if I knew Jonathan. He'd just about given up on Walter as a businessman."

"Don't be insulting, George," Mrs. Radford said coldly.

"Come now, Gertrude," Ames said. "Walter hates the idea of running the company, and you know it. Jonathan knew it, too, and he'll certainly have arranged it so that management will run the company at least for now. I hope so, anyway. I have a stake."

"Walter will prove he can run the company," Mrs. Radford said. "He'll take hold now. Deirdre will help once they are married."

"Perhaps she will at that," Ames said.

I said, "Miss Fallon and Walter are being married soon?"

"The announcement will be made after the funeral."

When I had first talked to George Ames, he had called Deirdre Fallon a "lady friend." Ames was a man I would have expected to be formal, and a fiancée is not a lady friend.

"A sudden decision?" I asked.

"No," Mrs. Radford said, "it was actually to be announced yesterday. That was what Deirdre discussed with Jonathan at lunch on Monday. Walter and Deirdre think we should wait longer, but I see no useful reason. We must balance death with life."

It was a nice speech that proved nothing. Had the late Jonathan maybe really opposed the marriage? It was a thought, but I wasn't going to find out here.

"Did Jonathan have a personal, private problem?" I asked.

"Good gracious no," Gertrude Radford said.

"Damn it, Fortune," George Ames said, "this Weiss came to collect money, Jonathan refused, and Weiss killed him. Those are the plain facts. You can't evade them."

"Why go to Jonathan?" I said. "Why not go to Walter?"

"Because Walter couldn't pay," Ames said testily. "Jonathan had control of his brother's estate until Walter was thirty."

Mrs. Radford said, "My husband did not believe that a woman could, or should, handle money. Except for a small income of my own, Jonathan controlled our money."

"What are you trying to find out, Fortune?" Ames said. "No one in the family was near the apartment at the time, except Gertrude, and she couldn't get in. She has no key. Jonathan was already dead then."

"Maybe," I said, "or maybe someone was with him keeping him quiet. Maybe he wasn't dead at two o'clock after all."

They didn't look startled, or guilty, they just stared at me with nothing to say to that.

I said, "Do any of you know a man named Paul Baron?"

"No."—"Of course not." They said together. Their ignorance sounded genuine. I dropped it.

"Where could I find Walter now?"

"He went out with Deirdre. She's staying in one of the cottages until the wedding," Mrs. Radford said. "We don't mean to be unhelpful, or callous, Mr. Fortune, but we can't help you. At the moment I am only concerned with binding our wounds."

"We all like to bind wounds," I said. "Thanks for seeing me."

None of the others drinking their ritual coffee had even glanced at me, and they didn't now as I walked out. I was an alien animal, some foreign species. They were behind their walls, and outside there were only strange breeds of no interest to them.

The butler ushered me out. The hour was almost up, so I stood in the biting night cold and waited for the taxi to return. I was thinking about Paul Baron and a world a lot different from the world of the Radfords, when I heard the light steps in the snow.

A thin shadow watched me from the trees at the corner of the house. The shadow hissed at me, said:

"Are you the detective?"

"Yes."

"Hurry," she said.

A female shadow that turned and walked away around the house. I followed.

7

THE PATH LED toward two cottages behind the house. Only one showed light. The tall woman led me toward the lighted one.

She wore boots, a loose one-piece wool dress, and nothing else against the ten-degree cold but an enormous red-and-white-striped scarf. She strode out like one of those old fanatics leading a crusade.

Inside, the main room of the cottage was bright and well-furnished. She led me through into a smaller room without even a glance at the expensive furniture. In the small room there were a narrow bed, straight chairs, two worn bureaus, an old desk piled with papers, and a shabby dining table. A monk's cell.

"Sit down," she said.

I sat. She sat at the desk. I saw her clearly, and she was a girl: a tall, lanky girl of about twenty-five, with a long solemn face.

"I'm Morgana. You're investigating Uncle Jonathan's death?"

"I suppose I am."

"You think someone here really killed him?"

"I don't think anything yet. Do you?"

"I think that a total stranger is a bit too convenient. My uncle was a strong and clever man. It strikes me that he was not a man to be killed so easily by someone who had come to squeeze money. He should have been alert in that situation."

That thought had crossed my mind. "Do you have an idea?"

She crossed her legs. It was an efficient, mannish gesture. She swung her booted leg as if she were about to give instructions to her soldiers. "No, not really. Any Radford or Ames is capable of murder, but I don't know of any motives. Logically there is my brother, Walter, but it couldn't have been Walter."

"Why not, and why logically?"

"He is basically too gentle to hurt anyone, although he hated Jonathan. Jonathan tried to make him a businessman, and Mother tried to make him a cold aristocrat. Because they both failed, they think he is weak, but it isn't that." Her leg swung faster to some inner conflict. "When we were both small, we took an oath to right the wrongs our family had done. To do only good. Mother and Jonathan destroyed that in Walter, but they could not make him what they wanted, so he became what he is."

"What is he?"

"Bitter, corrupt and self-indulgent." She looked at me. "But the gentle boy is still there; I know that. He couldn't kill."

"He has an alibi anyway. If he was really here on Monday."

"He was. I talked to him." Her leg swung. "But she wasn't."

"She?"

"The cool Deirdre. She gets it all now, you see?"

"Did Jonathan dislike her? Did he oppose her?"

"No, not at all. Jonathan admired her just as Mother does. They admired her strength. Good for Walter, they considered."

"Then why would she kill Jonathan?"

"There may be things I don't know. They don't tell me much."

"It's not logical for her to kill a man who liked her."

"Unless something had changed," Morgana Radford said. Her leg swung in spasms and her hands twitched. "There's something dark and animal in her. She looks at Walter like a spider."

"But she has an alibi. Everyone has an alibi."

She sighed. "I suppose so. I suppose it was this Weiss. In a way it is a kind of justice. Simple, stupid violence."

I watched her. "You didn't like your uncle, did you?"

Abruptly, she stood. She began to pace the Spartan room. "My uncle was an evil man. One of the evil Radfords! Do you know how the Radfords became powerful, rich? On blood! They called it coffee, but it was blood they sold. The blood of Indians, peasants, slaves! They robbed, killed and maimed the darker people of the world so that they could live in ease at home. It still goes on, day after day. Power, greed and self-interest, and Jonathan was the leader of today. A most efficient, strong man. I'm glad he's dead, and I won't let them make Walter like him!"

In her shapeless brown dress she looked like some fundamentalist preacher promising fire and brimstone. That's just what she was. A fanatic. What else she was, I couldn't say. Maybe she was on the edge of a private darkness, or maybe she was only a sensitive girl in a rapacious family. Fanatics do a lot of harm, but they do a lot of good, too. Maybe most of the good.

"Where were you on Monday, Miss Radford?"

"At work. I'm an officer in the Society of Economic Missions. Our work is to correct the wrongs of exploitation in colonial countries." She gave me an appraising look. She knew what I was asking. "It's in the East Fifties. I was there all morning. I came home on the train after Walter."

"Do you know about any problems your uncle had?"

She shook her head. "No, not really. I did hear Mother say once that Jonathan was becoming a night owl in his old age, but I don't know what it means. He did seem to take longer business trips recently."

"Night action and longer business trips? But you don't know if he was involved in something unusual for him?"

"No, but I wouldn't be surprised by anything Jonathan was involved in," Morgana Radford said bitterly. "Anything."

"Do you know where I can find Walter?"

"Probably at that Costa's gambling house. Jonathan closed it, but it opened up in the next town. Walter has to gamble, you see? He has to wallow. They did that to him."

She was no longer talking to me. I left her staring at what had to be some invisible image of Walter Radford. I went back to the house where my taxi waited in the snow. Mrs. Radford was there. "You were speaking to Morgana?"

"Yes."

She was silent a moment. In the forest some large night bird attacked a small animal. Mrs. Radford said, "She is a strange girl, withdrawn from us. It comes from having no father. She worshiped her only brother. She can't let him grow up, mature. She sees mature strength as evil."

There are always two sides, sometimes more, and all sides can be true. Strength can be mature. It can also be evil.

"Walter must assume charge now," Mrs. Radford said.

"I guess so, Mrs. Radford," I said. I was thinking that there were pressures in the Radford family. Whether they were a cause of Jonathan's death, or only a result, I had no way of knowing.

I got into the taxi. Mrs. Radford stood in the snow in front of the house and watched me leave.

Carmine Costa's casino was a big house on a back road with many small rooms inside. Some of the rooms were for relaxation and booze; six were for action. There were two roulette rooms, a dice room, a blackjack room, a baccarat layout, and a poker room. It was all open. No one cares much about other people gambling. In most police forces the vice squad is separate so that the other squads don't have to arrest the gamblers and girls they depend on for so much information that solves bigger crimes.

There was little of the frantic madness of Las Vegas. The people here had plenty of money to lose if that would help them to pass the time. Still, there were tense jaw muscles and sweaty palms hidden in dinner jacket pockets. No gambler wants to lose. Not once, not ever.

Deirdre Fallon stood at the dice table as slim as a crystal doll. A white evening dress that fitted her curves from ankle to high neck left no question this time about her hips and breasts. Her hand rested on the arm of a slender man beside her.

He was like his dead uncle, but younger and smaller. He held his body in an arrogant attitude, but the pallor of his face was almost anemic. His dinner jacket was flawless, and there was a superior tilt to his chin, but his eyes were dark circles with brown chips small in the center. His attention was totally on the dice game, and his mouth had a loose, petulant cast.

"Miss Fallon," I said.

She turned. "Are you following me, Mr. Fortune?"

"No, but it's a nice thought."

She wrinkled her nose at me, smiled. It gave me that twinge in my back. She touched the small man beside her.

"Walter. I think Mr. Fortune wants to talk to you."

He turned fast as if afraid he might respond too slowly and make Deirdre Fallon angry. His shadowed eyes scanned me. He did not like what he saw, and he was not a good enough actor to hide it. Or maybe he didn't give a damn.

"Fortune? You're working for that killer? Damn you, he killed my uncle for his blood money!"

"I thought it was Paul Baron's money?"

"Sure, Baron's money, but Weiss came crawling to get it! Why don't you find the money! Find it and you've got Weiss!"

His voice was loud, and people were looking at us. Deirdre Fallon put her arm around his thin waist.

"Walter is upset," she said. "He feels his uncle was killed because of him, and . . ."

He squirmed. "Deirdre, don't . . . !"

"It's the truth, Walter," she snapped.

"I know, damn it, but not to him!"

I was the alien, the outsider, in front of whom no Radford should ever drop the wall. Deirdre Fallon did not seem as worried about me. Maybe because she wasn't yet a Radford. She wasn't quite in the castle.

"Maybe you could tell me more about this money you owed to Paul Baron?" I said.

He seemed about to answer when the stickman tapped him. It was his turn to roll. He forgot me as if I had gone up in smoke. The dice were in his hands. His dull chip eyes shined. His mouth tightened, became firm, almost cruel. He was taller, as if he had gathered his muscles. He laid a hundred-dollar bill down.

"Shoot a hundred," he said in a smooth, cool voice that had taken on a faint British accent. He rolled a four.

"Four the point," the stickman droned. Hard point or easy, winner or loser, they were all suckers to the stickman.

"Another hundred rides on Little Joe," Walter said. Except he barked it like an officer ordering a bayonet charge.

He was a man at war. A soldier for glory and victory. A man like his ancestors battling heavy seas and steaming jungles. He thrilled to the battle, and it was the game that mattered, not the result. Maybe Deirdre Fallon could bring him out. Maybe no one had ever helped him to find anything worth fighting for.

Deirdre Fallon was watching me. "You look disapproving."

"A man has to get his kicks," I said. "I guess Walters One, Two and Three were gamblers, too."

"You don't like the suggestion of aristocracy in the numbers?"

"I'm not much impressed by family. My grandfather would have been. He was arrogant about being a Fortunowski of Poland."

She smiled a nice, open smile. "I would have liked your grandfather. Family is important in a chaotic world."

"If the family has values."

"The Radfords have many values. Mostly good ones. Walter simply hasn't found the right values for himself yet."

"And you mean to help him find them?"

She smiled again. "Perhaps reshaping men is a disease of women, but Walter loves me, and I'm going to like being a Radford."

Before I could answer that one, Walter crapped out. I saw him deflate as the pot was raked away and the dice passed. His eyes were deep pools of loss. It wasn't the pot he stared at, it was the dice in another man's hands.

Deirdre Fallon took his arm. "We can have a drink and talk."

His sorrowful eyes looked at her. It was as naked a look as I had ever seen. His whole face said that the dice were gone and there was nothing left in the universe for him but Deirdre Fallon. What more could a woman ask? Especially when wealth, position, and maybe even power went with it?

I followed them into one of the lounge rooms. Deirdre Fallon ordered for all of us: martinis for them, an Irish for me.

"You wanted to know about Paul Baron, Mr. Fortune?" she said.

"I wondered how Walter lost so much to him."

"By playing bad poker over quite a few months," Walter said. He had changed again. He was more open, direct, a pleasant young man. He was something of a chamelon, changeable. "Paul was always very nice about accepting my markers."

"How did you meet him?"

"When my uncle closed Costa, I was shut off everywhere in Westchester. They were all afraid of Jonathan. So I moved into New York and met Baron at a party about seven months ago."

"Sammy Weiss, too?"

"I met Weiss twice. He hung around some bigger games Baron took me to. I usually played in small games at Paul's East Sixteenth Street apartment. I told him I'd pay the $25,000 in installments. I thought he had agreed. I told him that Jonathan wouldn't pay."

"You didn't know he was sending Weiss to collect?"

"No. I'd never have let him."

"Did your uncle know Weiss was only a messenger?"

"I don't know. I didn't tell Jonathan about the money this time. Paul must have contacted him directly."

"How did you plan to pay even in installments? From what I hear, you don't have any money like $25,000."

Deirdre Fallon said, "I don't see how that matters."

"I don't know what does matter yet," I said.

"I hoped to float small loans," Walter said. "I'm twenty-nine; there was less than a year before I got all my father's money anyway.

People will lend on that even with my record. Baron just wouldn't wait! He had to send Weiss, and Weiss killed my uncle!"

Deirdre Fallon said, "I'm sorry for your friend Weiss. I'm sure he didn't mean to kill Jonathan, but he did."

"He's no friend, and he's a cheap hustler, but I can't see him as a killer. Was Jonathan involved in anything shady?"

Walter laughed. "Not Jonathan."

Deirdre Fallon didn't answer me. She was watching something behind me. I turned. Two men in dinner jackets stood over us. The taller of them had an easy smile aimed at Miss Fallon.

"Mr. Costa," she said.

Carmine Costa bowed. "Miss Fallon, Mr. Radford, nice to have you back. Gives the place class."

Costa was big, dark and handsome. He had broad shoulders and a narrow waist; clean hands and thick dark hair and snapping black eyes. He seemed to paw the ground like a stallion as he looked at Deirdre Fallon.

"Nothing could do that," she said with contempt in her voice, "but at least you don't cheat, or do you?"

"For you I'd cheat myself."

"You're a pig, Mister Costa," she said.

He put his hand on her shoulder and moved it up to her neck. "A boar, Miss Fallon. A wild old boar."

She looked up into his face, and then reached up with both hands and gripped his wrist as if to pull the hand away. For a second or two she just held the wrist. Walter Radford moved.

"Get your hands off her!" Walter said, and swung at Costa's face.

The other man with Costa moved like a snake. His hand caught Walter's wrist before it had gone four inches. Costa barked:

"Strega!"

The man, Strega, dropped Walter's wrist and stepped back as if he had never moved. I had never seen anyone move so fast. Strega was not as tall as Costa, not as broad, seemed quieter in his dinner jacket, and yet there was no question which of the two was the stronger man. Strega was blond and smooth and there were no marks on his Nordic face, but he seemed to exude pure power. The muscleman, the bodyguard.

Costa bowed. "My mistake, no offense to the lady. Strega, apologize to Mr. Radford."

Strega inclined his head. "Mr. Radford."

"Sure," Walter Radford said. "Okay, Deirdre?"

She nodded. "Mr. Costa can't help his bad manners. He probably intended a compliment. But we better leave, Walter."

I watched her lead Walter out. Costa watched her, too.

"There's a woman," Costa said. "Right, Strega?"

"Some woman, Sarge," Strega said.

Costa became aware of me. "You want something?"

"A little talk," I said, "about Jonathan Radford."

Costa eyed me. "Sure, why not? Come in the office."

I followed him toward a curtained doorway.

Strega followed me.

8

COSTA'S OFFICE was modest and had no windows. Airconditioning hummed, the safe was a vault only an army could crack, the chairs were leather, and the desk was steel and small.

"Sit down," Costa said.

I started for a chair. Strega's hands frisked me from behind with a delicate touch and no wasted motion. Costa sat behind his desk and waited.

"Okay," Strega said.

I sat. The bodyguard walked away to a corner. He made no noise as he walked. Strega was the new-style bodyguard, what they call now a "show-guard." He could go anywhere and blend in—a society party, a political dinner, a ladies' tea.

"No iron?" Costa said. "That's smart. Guns win battles, brains win wars, right?"

"Lawyers win wars," I said. "Our kind of wars."

"You got a point. Who are you?"

"Dan Fortune. A private detective."

Costa closed his eyes, leaned back. "Fortune? Yeh, wait now . . . wait . . . Danny the Pirate, sure. Chelsea. I was East New York." He opened his eyes. "You're small beans, baby."

"Real small," I agreed. "You're East New York? Profaci's family, or the Gallo boys?"

"To hell with that. I do business, sure, but that's all."

Profaci was the former Mafia leader of Brooklyn. He had been a tough leader—so tough he had died of natural causes. The Gallos were Profaci's enemies. What Costa was saying was that he was an independent, not Mafia. He looked as if it meant something to him. His dark eyes considered my missing arm.

"The war?" he asked.

"I never made it."

"Too bad. I was master sergeant. In the Big Red One. We made the landings, baby. We pushed the Krauts back on their cans. Real war, real soldiers. When you got that behind you, you don't cozy up to punks like the Mafia. There ain't one of them wouldn't have fainted in a real war, and that goes for Charley Lucky, too. Without guns they couldn't handle an old ladies' bridge club, and with the guns they can't hit the *Queen Mary* at fifty feet. They got to use choppers to hit a parked car. They shoot guys in the head 'cause they got to get that close or miss. The bosses can't walk into a bar without six punks casing it first."

"You don't need a bodyguard?"

"Strega? He's my friend, baby. He was infantry, too, in Korea. We're a team, only I can handle myself. I hit the bull six out of seven with an automatic at fifty yards. I can take any man with my hands, short of a bigger professional and Strega. With me and Strega it's a draw. Right, Strega?"

Strega leaned in the corner, his eyes blank. "I'll take you sixty-forty, Sarge. With an automatic, you got the edge."

Costa laughed. Strega was serious. The quick brains were probably with Costa, he was the boss, but I'd rather have met him in an alley than Strega. Beyond that they were two of a kind: self-contained and self-sufficient. Proud. They bowed to no man. It was almost refreshing in our organization world.

Costa said, "What do you want to know about Radford?"

"What can you tell me?"

"You want to know if I knocked him off? Because he closed me down over in North Chester?"

"It's a reason," I said.

"No it isn't, baby. It's all in the game. I shut the nephew off cold and opened here. No sweat." He leaned back again, fixed those dark eyes on me. "We don't kill people anymore, not outside the club. Sure, inside the boys still hit each other sometimes, but not outside. Too much pressure now. Anastasia gets it, the cops cheer. Knock off a citizen, and you got trouble. If the citizen was a big wheel, the trouble is so bad no fix works, and that's bad for business."

"And Radford was important?"

"You know it. Talk about Mafia, but, baby, they're nothing compared to a guy like Jonathan Radford. He was real power. The connections, the influence, the real muscle. If he looks sideways at the cops, no fix could stick. He calls the Governor, he gets troopers and maybe the national guard. Congress listens to him. The President talks to him. He was a corporation, baby, with a reach went everywhere. I did what he didn't like. He made a phone call and I was out of business. No threats, no guns, no muscle. That's power, baby. He closed me to show he wanted the kid shut off. I shut the kid off. He let me open here."

"Sometimes a man gets squeezed so hard he just has to stand up and fight no matter how bad the odds," I said.

Costa scowled now. "Listen, baby. He wanted me out of North Chester, and I got out. He didn't even talk to me. Guys like him think guys like me and you ain't even human. If they need us, they use us like they'd use a dog. If they don't need us, they don't even see us as long as we keep out of their way. I stay open, baby, only because guys like Radford are too busy to worry about me, and the good citizens don't care."

"Probably true and logical," I said, "but you don't strike me as a man who's always logical."

He grinned. "Anyway, baby, I've got me an alibi. Soon as I heard, I knew the cops'd be around. They came. I told them what I'm telling you: me and Strega was in the city early Monday, sure, but we was back here by one o'clock. We got proof. Okay?"

"Okay," I said. "Did you hear about Jonathan being mixed up in anything?"

"No, but what would I hear about what he did?"

"Do you know a man named Paul Baron?"

"I heard of him, but I never met the man. We work different streets. He's a con artist, a sharpie. I'm a businessman. Him and his women work badger games; play the ships, the resorts. His kind'll try to take a casino as fast as any private mark. I'd throw him out."

"Walter Radford lost $25,000 to Baron at poker."

Costa whistled. "Walter can't play, but Baron probably cold-decked him, too. Only $25,000 is damned high for a loner like Baron to let the tab go."

"I was thinking that myself," I agreed. "Maybe Baron sort of knew Walter was going to be rich soon. I notice Walter isn't shut off here anymore."

"The old man's dead. No worries now," Costa said. "Walter's loaded, if the Fallon doesn't queer the deal when she marries him. Except I don't give that two years before she wants out, or maybe he does. She's got too much class for him."

"You like her?"

"There's something in her, baby. Only you saw she won't give me the time of day. Not now. Maybe later."

"Keep hoping," I said, and stood up.

"I will, baby."

I left Costa with a faraway look in his black eyes. Strega still leaned in his corner, a statue. But just as I reached the door, the blond man's gray eyes turned to look at me. Intense gray eyes, as if Strega wanted to be sure to remember my face.

Outside the casino in the cold I lighted a cigarette. The stars were clear and hard. It had been a day of the wild goose, and no help to Sammy Weiss. I decided to have one more go at finding Weiss, and maybe Paul Baron. The cops should have given up on Weiss's room by now. Maybe I could find some lead they had missed.

9

ST. MARKS PLACE is one of those streets that make New York what it is. It is in what was once called the Ghetto, where the great Yiddish culture flourished. The Jews still live in the area, but now the Poles are there, the Ukrainians, the Italians, and a host of other peoples. The bums are there because the Bowery is near. The artists are there because it is also the East Village, the present cheap Bohemia. The alienated are there, and the grotesque. Old and young; middle-class and far out; bearded hippie and bearded Chassidim; black, white, yellow and brown. All walk in relative peace.

On any given block between Third Avenue and Avenue A there may be a Polish Hall, a Slovenian Roman Catholic Church, an Italian café, a *Bodega-Carniceria*, and a Jewish restaurant. There are lower-middle-class tenements, flophouse hotels, apartments with doormen, and some of the lowest rooming houses anywhere. There are spit-and-sawdust workmen's bars, psychedelic coffee houses, and three places where you can buy marijuana over the counter.

At the moment, St. Marks Place itself is a hippie heaven, a far-out Coney Island of the flower-children and the LSD-trippers. Every night is Mardi Gras on this year's St. Marks Place. It will not always be this. It will change again with the city and life itself, and no one can say what it will be tomorrow.

And underneath the surface carnival of today, the old Ghetto, Bowery, and melting pot still holds firm, offering a home to men like Sammy Weiss, who have never known peace and who love only the dollar made without work.

Weiss's room was on the third floor rear, and it was not locked. I went in with caution. The room was empty. With its nameless furniture, greasy stove, and sagging bed, it looked like it had always been empty. The single closet held one suit, one pair of slacks, and one worn pair of shoes. In the bureau there was underwear, socks, and a strange article that seemed to be an old male corset. There were two clean shirts with turned collars.

All men, petty gambler or king, are much the same day to day. I could picture Weiss, of the fur collar and big bluff, alone in this room turning his shirt collars and hoping that a corset would make him slim and young again before he gave up and let his pot sag.

I found nothing. Only the evidence of a small and empty life. There were only some twenty-seven miles between this room and North Chester, but it was hard to believe that the two places held members of the same species.

I heard the door open. I looked up to see a man come in and lean against the door. A gray man, tall and slender.

"Hello, Fortune."

He wore a gray cashmere overcoat, pale gray gloves, and his gray trousers draped perfectly to shined black shoes. He wore his gray Homburg at too much angle, and his handsome face had an edge of anxiety he would never completely hide. It added up to only one conclusion—a man who lived by wits and guile, and for whom clothes, pleasures and the best places were not by-products of life but ends in themselves. A con man.

"What do you want to make waves for, Fortune?"

"Looking for Weiss is making waves?" I said.

"Big waves," he said.

"You're Paul Baron?"

He had an odd way of looking at some point on a far wall. He looked at a wall and nodded. "I'm Paul Baron. You're getting in my way, Fortune."

"Enough to be pushed under a train?"

Baron considered the ceiling. "That was a bad play. Spur-of-the-moment, you know how it is. It seemed like an idea at the time."

"What is it?" I said, and stepped toward Baron. "You want to silence Sammy before he can finger you for killing Radford?"

I suppose I stepped toward him to show him that I wasn't afraid of him. If I did, it worked fine, but not with exactly the result I had had in mind.

Baron said, "Leo."

A second man appeared in the open doorway. A short, broad man with enormous, dangling hands, and massive shoulders like the hump of a bull buffalo. He shambled into the room on short, stiff legs that seemed to have no knees, and watched me with blank-faced concentration.

Baron studied a stain on the far wall. "Now listen good, Danny boy, and then forget what you heard. A man owed me money. I'm an easy-going man, but I like to be paid. This man couldn't pay me, but he had an uncle who could. I sent Sammy Weiss to collect my money. Weiss got my money, but I didn't get it. I still don't have my money. I want it."

Baron let a silence hover in the room as if to give his point time to sink in. I could hear the rasping breathing of Leo the buffalo.

I said, "You know, it's strange, but I'm having trouble seeing Sammy Weiss with the nerve to cross you."

Baron sighed. "Let's try it once more, okay? I sent Weiss for my money. Something went wrong, I guess, and Sammy panicked. He killed Radford. I don't care about that. But it seems like Sammy figured if he had to run he could use $25,000 to pay his way. That I care about. Now you go ahead and help Weiss on the murder rap, but after I get my money. Right now I don't need you nosing around. Check?"

"The money is evidence in a murder, Baron."

"Sure. That's why I need it before anyone finds Weiss. I'm doing Sammy a favor. They won't find the money on him."

"You're sure they'd find it on him now?"

He looked straight at me for the first time. His eyes were pale gray like the rest of him. Barbarian eyes under the veneer.

"You're a bug, Fortune. A hard-head bug. Leo!"

The buffalo-man was on me before I could even start to think of moving. He was behind me with my arm in one hand and the back of my neck in the other. My neck isn't thin, but Leo's hand held it like a clamp on a pipe. Baron stepped to me.

He took a hypodermic syringe from his pocket. Leo held me as immobile as a strait jacket. And Leo had more than muscle; he knew what he was doing. He held me so that if I moved hard my arm would break, and maybe my neck.

I looked at the syringe and wondered if this was my last day. I didn't want it to be my last day. Not now, not ever. But there was nothing I could do. I had no chance at all to fight. None. Like a Jew going to the gas chamber. That is a terrible moment.

"Just relax, Danny boy," Baron said.

He rolled up my sleeve and shot me in the vein. He grinned into my face and massaged my arm. I waited. Leo's grip did not relax. After a time I felt the sleep coming. I hoped it was sleep.

When my knees sagged, Leo picked me up and laid me on the bed. I raised up and swung at a shadow. I hit empty air. Something pushed me back flat on the bed. I breathed.

Leo leaned close. A hand slapped my face, hard. Leo went away. He had not spoken once. Maybe he didn't know how.

I hoped it was sleep.

I lay in dim light on something flat. I saw a window high in a gray wall. There was darkness beyond the window. A barred window. I saw a washbasin and a toilet. Only three walls. The fourth wall was vertical bars.

I sat up. I stood up. My legs were shaky. I wondered what Baron had fed me. It had the feel of morphine. I didn't want to think about why it had been morphine. I sat down again to let my legs steady and my head clear. The cell looked like a precinct cell. I reached for a cigarette. I had none. The men in the other cells heard me moving.

"Hey, junkie, you gonna get hung."

I had the urge to get up and pace. I resisted. The one thing you never do in a cell is pace. Every minute would become an hour. What you do is lie flat and think about something with many, many small parts—like a walking trip across the city, step by step.

"Sweat, junkie!"

Everyone has to hate something. But the shouts told me that I had been found on Weiss's bed with the syringe and makings. In another cell a man began to whistle flat and off key. Voices echoed:

"Shut up! . . . For Chrissake shut it off! . . ."

Somewhere someone began to cry. I wondered how good a fix Baron had hung on me. I guessed that he had not wanted to kill me because of the risk. A push under a train is one thing, a killing in a room where Baron could be placed is another. The whistler down the corridor didn't stop. Detective Freedman was at my cell door before I heard him.

"You got real trouble now, Fortune."

"I'm no junkie. You know it's a frame."

"We found you with all the equipment and knocked out on M. It's good enough. Where's Sammy Weiss?"

"I don't know."

"Hiding a fugitive is a bad charge."

"Trying to find one isn't."

"Don't try to be a hard guy. Tell me about Weiss."

"I haven't seen him since Monday night. I turned him away, told him to give himself up. I guess he had his own ideas."

"You turned down his money?"

"He didn't have money. He was broke."

"He told you that?"

"Yes. Weiss is always broke."

"You believe he's broke now?"

What did I say? I didn't know if I believed Weiss was broke or not. It looked like he was far from broke.

"Where is he, Fortune?"

"I still don't know. And in here I'm not going to find out."

Freedman watched me for a time before he turned and vanished. He hadn't used his fists. That made me wonder. I could think of only two reasons why Bert Freedman would hold back on his fists: he was sure the drug charge would hold up, and I would tell all soon; or he had orders from higher up that they were interested in me.

I thought about both possibilities for a long time. I didn't sleep much. No one came near me. The off-key whistling went on. Other men complained. Men coughed. It was a long night.

They got us up early, let us scratch and dab water in our eyes, fed us, and marched us to the paddy wagon. The wagon drove us through a gray dawn city in bitter cold. We hunched, and hawked, and spat, and coughed. (Even one night in jail and you begin to think not as "I" but as "we.")

At Centre Street we were herded into Headquarters fast as if they were afraid that our collection of drunks, bums, and petty crooks was planning a daring escape with the aid of gunmen hidden behind every parked car. We waited in the bullpen behind the line-up stage. No one talked. For the detectives with us, the line-up was an annoying duty too early in the day. For us prisoners it was the final moment of hope; the last chance.

Ninety percent of prisoners each day are small, habitual law-breakers. Once arraigned and charged, they know the rest by heart. They can tell you the result of the trial, and the sentence, the instant they are charged before a judge. So it is the line-up they face uneasily. The line-up is where they can still hope for release, where maybe they will still walk away free for one more day. And as each name is called, they shuffle up the steps onto the stage, nervous and with hopeful eyes. For ninety-nine out of a hundred it is a feeble hope.

My turn came, and Freedman pushed me up the four steps. I stood out under the bright lights with my head just reaching the five-foot-ten mark. It is an unnerving experience. You can never know what you look like to other people, and on that stage you know you look guilty of every crime there is.

"This specimen is Daniel Fortune," the interrogating officer of the day announced.

I recognized the voice. It was Captain Gazzo.

10

GAZZO TALKED to the audience, "Fortune was picked up on a tip. He was under morphine, the tools around him. He . . ."

I thought about that game they play on television: *To Tell the Truth*. It is the line-up made into amusement for the millions. Something is wrong with people who make the pain of the line-up into a parlor game. When a man is in the line-up, he is trying to save his existence. If he lies, it is because he is desperate, because he faces pain and the terror of a cell. On the TV show a man lies for applause and a prize. If he lies well, he feels important. It makes you wonder.

"Tell us about it, Fortune," Grazzo said.

I told them about the frame, and about my search for Weiss, but I left out Baron's story about Weiss and the $25,000. I heard them breathing out there. Most of them were police, professional and detached, but some were ordinary citizens. The public. The gray monster. Not because they were mean or vicious, but because they don't know, they are in the dark. They cannot know the pain of the single stranger up on the stage. That is not an accusation; it is a fact. We are all part of the gray monster until, by some stroke of chance, we are up there alone on the stage.

"Fortune has no history of junk," Gazzo explained to the audience. "He's got no yellow sheet. He's a private detective, when he works at it. He's also been a seaman, waiter, tourist guide, farmhand, laborer, actor, student, sometime journalist, and God knows what else. A middle-age roustabout. I doubt if he ever made enough to support even a small habit. How come you never work hard, Fortune?"

"I never found the work, Captain."

I never found work worth doing for its own sake. The best I found is trying to solve other people's problems. I've talked to people all over the world, and not many could ever tell me, simply and with conviction, why they work at what they do, why they went into their work, or what they get out of it. Most gave me a three-hour sales talk full of overenthusiasm and too many words. A lot just stared at me. They seemed mystified. No one had ever asked them why they worked at their work, and they had obviously never asked themselves. Maybe they were afraid to ask themselves.

"All right, Fortune, step down."

Usually a prisoner is ordered to Felony Court, or Magistrates Court, or some such disposition. Gazzo gave no instructions on me, so I knew that where I was going had been arranged in advance. That was good to know. It meant that Gazzo and the others had only been softening me up.

I was taken across to the Annex by a detective who made no show of guarding me. In Gazzo's office the detective left me to wait with Gazzo's female sergeant. She is pretty, but I never had learned her name. Gazzo doesn't really know her name. He never married, and women make him nervous. I waited an hour in silence and cigarette smoke.

"Inside," Gazzo said when he arrived.

I sat in the dim midnight of Gazzo's inner office, and it was hard to believe that it was early morning out in the winter city. Gazzo watched me from behind his desk. He is a hard man who has lived long enough in a hard world to leave the obvious hardness to others. An eager man no longer eager to punish.

"I had enough to cool you a week, Dan."

"I know," I said. "You can get to business, Captain."

"You've been busy," Gazzo said. "Upper East Side, Lower East, the Village, Westchester. All for Sammy Weiss?"

"Why not for Weiss?"

"You're not that close to him. Did he pay you big?"

"He didn't pay me at all."

"You're sure, Dan?"

It was a serious question. Gazzo had a special reason for wanting to know if Weiss had paid me. Something more than whether or not Sammy had money or I could be bought. I let it slide. If he wanted me to know, he would tell me.

"I'm sure," I said, and then I told him what I had done, except for my trip to the morgue and Baron's story. I told him about George Ames, the North Chester people, Carmine Costa, and what I knew of the murder.

"Weiss said he hit Radford and left him alive?" Gazzo said.

"That's what he said. About one-thirty."

"So we know that Radford was alive at one-fifteen when Weiss got there. I wasn't sure of that. The doorman saw him at one. We only had the Fallon girl's word for one-fifteen. Now Weiss agrees."

"He was alive when Sammy left at one-thirty, too."

"According to Weiss only. Mrs. Radford got no answer at two. We know she had no key, and there wasn't time for her to get in, kill Radford, and still get back down in time for the doorman to see her when he did."

Gazzo rubbed his stubble. "Everyone in the family is clear from around noon until past three o'clock. We haven't found any suspects in Radford's private or business life. If Weiss didn't kill him, we've got fifty minutes for someone else to get in, kill, and get out unseen. And we've got no reasonable suspect."

"The sister, Morgana, suspects Deirdre Fallon."

"Swell. Only she's got an alibi, and not much motive."

"The engagement is pretty sudden."

"They all agree Jonathan liked her. What does she gain?"

"Walter is the prime suspect to me," I said. "He needed money, he was on a leash that pinched, he had most to gain, and he's a weak, arrogant type who probably never knows what he'll do."

"He's been all that for a lot of years," Gazzo said. "Why does he kill with less than a year to wait for his money?"

"Paul Baron."

"Walter was squeezed before; he never killed."

"The uncle wouldn't pay this time. He admits that."

"It's not enough, not with just a year to go. Anyway, show me how Walter kills from North Chester and I'll book him."

"What about the weapon?"

"Looks like a souvenir Malay kris Jonathan had on his desk. It's missing." Gazzo's gray eyes jabbed through me. "Okay, sure, it was crazy for anyone to take the knife, but that's just what a panicky killer might do. We all know Weiss wouldn't plan a murder, but he's just the type to grab the knife out of fear, and then run with it. Too scared to stop and wipe the knife, but just smart enough to know his prints would be on it. Panic."

I changed direction. "What do you know about Paul Baron?"

"Everything, including that we have nothing against him, unless you want to make a charge." Gazzo grinned. He knew I had no charge that could stick. When I said nothing, he went on, "After Walter Radford told us it was Baron he really owed the money to, we looked for Baron. He came in on his own late last night. After he worked on you, I guess. We talked to him. He said he'd sent Weiss for his money. He said Weiss never came back. He admitted he was looking for Weiss. He had an alibi for the time of the murder."

"What alibi?"

Gazzo spoke straight-faced. "A singer-dancer at the Fifth Street Club, Misty Dawn, was with him until one o'clock at her place. A girl named Carla Devine was with him from about one-thirty until past six o'clock. He's a lady-chaser. We talked to both women; they back him."

"You're kidding," I said. "Who's the Devine girl?"

"Call her a B-girl if you want. She keeps rich men happy when they come to town. She lives with four other girls in an apartment on University Place. Baron hangs around the place. The girls work for themselves, but Baron drums up contacts."

"Hell, they're both in his pocket."

"Give me some proof they're lying."

"I'm pretty sure I saw Misty Dawn with Weiss about eight P.M. Monday. They got into a cab together. Which means Baron is probably lying when he says Weiss never came back to him."

"Not necessarily. At that time Baron didn't know Radford was dead. Weiss probably gave the Dawn woman the slip after you saw them, and then Baron started chasing Weiss."

I lighted a cigarette. "You know, Gazzo, Baron's a sharp con man, yet he's supposed to have let Walter Radford get into him for $25,000 when Walter couldn't pay."

"You think the money wasn't a poker debt?"

"Baron's known more for con games, the squeeze. He works with women, the badger games. No capital, just some polite blackmail. A payoff is more in his line."

"Does it matter, Dan?" Gazzo said. "Whatever it was for, the uncle wouldn't pay, and that got him killed."

"I think it matters. It changes the degree of pressure. It's no longer a one-shot $25,000. Motives get changed," I said. "When Weiss came to me, he was worried, but he wasn't scared to death. He tried to buy an alibi. He wouldn't have done that if the charge was murder. He'd have run and never stopped."

"So?"

"So I don't think he knew Radford was dead then. He'd never have tried to buy me on a murder rap; I wouldn't stay bought. No, I'll swear he didn't know Radford was dead."

"So he didn't know the man was dead. So what?"

"He couldn't have known there was even a chance Radford was dead, stabbed, and he couldn't have stolen $25,000. Damn it, by coming to me he admitted he was there with Radford. It was as good as a confession. No, his story to me was true. If it hadn't been, he'd have taken the money and dug to China, just the way he's doing now that he's really scared."

Gazzo ticked off, "Witnesses already placed him there. He didn't think he could buy you; he just wanted to get his story on record so you could tell it later and create doubt. When you didn't seem convinced, then he ran for China." Gazzo leaned back in his chair. "You're talking logic, Dan; what a rational man would do and not do. A scared punk like Weiss could do anything. I'd be a lot more doubtful Weiss is our man if he was supposed to have acted smart and rational."

I stood up. "Can I leave?"

"Anytime."

I watched his face. "I'll say it again, Captain: you won't look for anyone while you've got Weiss in hand. You won't even try. They won't let you up top. But I can look."

"Don't buck us, Dan."

I walked out. I didn't even feel as good as I should have walking out after a night in jail. I was mad. Sammy Weiss was no one, nothing. He belonged in some jail. What did it matter if maybe there was some doubt this time?

11

BEFORE I DROPPED in bed, I called my part-time answering service. Weiss might have heard I was looking around and tried to contact me. It was a forlorn hope. In Chelsea people are wary of the telephone. There was no message from Weiss, but a lady had called once: no name and no number.

I set my alarm for one o'clock and collasped in the bed. I thought about the nameless lady, but not for long. Marty would have left her name. I thought about Weiss. Where was he? How was he keeping on the loose? Almost three days with half the New York police looking for him. Someone had to be helping him. I went to sleep thinking that $25,000 buys a lot of help.

The telephone woke me up. My head said I had slept an hour. The clock said it was almost noon. I fumbled with the receiver and managed to mumble something like "Hello?"

"Mr. Fortune?" a woman's voice asked. Her voice was low and throaty.

"I think so," I said. "Let me check."

"You're working on the murder of Jonathan Radford?"

"Hold on," I said. "I'll be back."

I put down the receiver and went into the bathroom. I doused sleep and morphine hangover from my head in cold water. I came out, lighted a cigarette, and picked up the telephone.

"Who is this?" I asked.

"My name is Agnes Moore," she said, low and quiet. "I'd like to talk to you. There could be money in it."

"What about Radford?"

"We'll talk. Come to 17 West Seventy-sixth Street. Top floor."

She hung up. I finished my cigarette. Then I took a shower. I wondered if Sammy Weiss had found a devious way to contact me. Someone had to be hiding him. On the other hand, I'd be careful where I walked. When I was dressed, I went out and to the subway.

At Seventy-second Street a thin haze hung over the Park like damp smoke, and lights were on in the tall buildings even in the early afternoon. The feel of more snow was in the air, and it was not so cold. Number 17 on Seventy-sixth Street was the usual brownstone. I rang. The door buzzed to let me in.

The stairs were carpeted and clean, and the wood of the walls shined as I went up. The door of the top apartment was painted black, and had an elegant brass knocker. I used the knocker. She answered at once.

"Come in, Mr. Fortune."

She was just over medium height. She wore a loose red kimono that swept the floor. Her dark hair was cut short in Italian curls, and her round face was pretty in a scrubbed, mannish way. She was around thirty, give or take, and she looked as if she had just stepped from the shower.

I went inside warily and braced for action.

"Sit down," she said.

The living room was large for the West Side. The furniture was good and expensive, but oddly impersonal. It looked like a matched set bought complete by someone who had said, "Wrap up the room and send it home." A model room in a good department store with none of the clutter that piles up after a time of living.

I sat. "How do you know about me, Miss Moore?"

"I have friends, and you're easy to spot." She nodded at my empty sleeve.

"What friends? Maybe Sammy Weiss?"

"I don't know Weiss, and what friends doesn't matter. I want to talk about the murder, isn't that enough?"

Her low voice was strong. It reminded me of someone else: Misty Dawn, or Deirdre Fallon, or Morgana Radford. I was collecting contralto females. Maybe it was the New York winter.

"How do you fit with Jonathan Radford, Miss Moore?"

"Close," she said, and laughed. "I was his girl friend, or lover; you name it how you like."

Her diction was good, but an uneducated past lurked behind her voice. She was relaxed, but there was a hardness in her that comes from growing up fast where life was not easy. I knew now why Jonathan Radford had become a night owl, and where the long business trips had taken him—to this apartment.

"Full time, or do you do something else?"

"I make my living acting. I support myself, but Jonathan liked me, and I liked him. He set up this place. He made life nicer for me, and I made it nicer for him. Check?"

"Check. Why the cloak-and-sneak, then? You were both adults."

"It wasn't so undercover. He came on the hush-hush only when he was involved with business and family in town here, and when I wasn't living here. We'd meet for a few good hours. But when he was freer, or officially out of town, and when I could stay here a while, we'd spend a week or more here."

"Why don't you live here? Husband?"

She reached for a cigarette from a gold box. She lighted it, stood up, and went to a home bar. She glided in the red kimono. She poured a snifter of Remy Martin cognac and looked at me. I nodded. She poured one for me, handed it down, and sat down again. "I'd say that was my business. I want to hire you to find who killed Jonathan, not tell you my life history.'"

"A husband is my business if he's the jealous type."

She smoked, drank. "Okay, I buy that. I've got no husband and no jealous boy friends. I don't live here because I have a lot of men friends I need in business. If they had known about Jonathan, it would have scared them off. In show business it helps a woman to be unattached and have a cozy place where men relax."

"Was that why Jonathan was discreet, too? To cover you?"

"Hell, no. That was for his family and business associates. We made nice music, but we had different lives. We agreed on no strings and no public hand-holding. He never asked me what I did away from him, and I respected his problems. I didn't fit into his public life. I'd have told some Senator he was a crook, and asked an ambassador if his wife was as frigid as she looked."

"Why do you want to hire me?"

"His family will read the will, bury him, and forget him. They won't care who killed him, the family goes on. Well, I care who killed him. I want the killer to take a big fall. For your record, I'm not in his will. He left me plenty, but in cash in my hands, so I didn't have to kill him. I was in my other place all Monday morning. I can't prove it; I was alone."

"Okay," I said. "The cops have Weiss convicted. If you want to rent me, you must have some other ideas."

"One. A man named Paul Baron was trying to extort money from Jonathan over something Jonathan's nephew had done."

"Extort? Not collect a debt?"

"Extort is what Jonathan said." She drained her brandy. "The nephew was mixed up in a racket with some B-girls. He set up dates between rich guys he knew and the girls. He got paid. Baron had pictures, checks, witnesses."

It makes a man feel good to have guessed right. I hadn't liked the gambling debt all along. Maybe there had been a debt, but only as a wedge for some kind of setup. It sounded like some cute variation on the badger game. That fitted Baron's M.O.

"Jonathan pays, or Baron goes to the cops," she said. "Jonathan was purple. He said he wouldn't even talk to Baron. The last time I saw him, Saturday, he said Walter could rot."

"He must have changed his mind, at least about talking to Paul Baron," I said. "How did you meet him in the first place?"

"I worked a TV show with George Ames. I met Jonathan. Bang!"

"Did Jonathan mention anyone else in the blackmail besides Baron?"

"No, but there had to be some girls, right? And it sure looks to me like the nephew and his girl had plenty to lose."

"Did Jonathan ever mention a Carmine Costa?"

"The guy he had closed up in North Chester? Sure. That was another of Walter's little games."

"Did he say anything else about Costa? Was there trouble?"

"Just that he closed him down."

"All right," I said. "Now do you want to tell me who told you about me?"

"No one. I've been sort of watching Jonathan's apartment. I saw you. You're easy to describe. I found out."

"I'm still working for Sammy Weiss, too."

"Just find that killer. That's all I want."

She became silent. I watched her stare at a big chair to my right. His chair, I figured. It was the first hint of sentiment I had seen in her. She came out of it:

"How much will you want now?"

Jonathan had left her plenty, according to her. I said, "A hundred a day and expenses. Three days now."

She gave me a stare. I saw that she knew it was steep for a small-timer like me. But she went to her desk and came back with three hundred-dollar bills. She wanted the killer bad. She also wanted something else.

"Keep me out of it, right?" she said.

"If I can," I said.

I left her drinking more brandy and looking at that big chair.

On the subway I felt a lot better. I had three hundred dollars, a client, and some real motives for murder. Money had been a thin motive for the Radford crowd, but the threat of dirty publicity, a messy trial, and jail wasn't so thin. Only the Radfords still all had alibis.

I liked Paul Baron more, and now he had a solid motive. Maybe Jonathan had changed his mind about seeing or talking to Baron because he intended to blow the whistle. Costa was right: Jonathan Radford had been real power. Paul Baron might have realized that he had bitten off more than he could handle, and had needed to cover up. Baron's alibi was pure smog. Both his witnesses were probably involved in the blackmail up to their girlish smiles.

All the way to my office I thought about calling Gazzo with my new information, but I wasn't sure I had enough, so when I got to my desk I called my answering service first.

It was my day. When a case begins to crack, it sometimes opens up everywhere at once. My service had a message this time. Sammy Weiss had called at last. He wanted to see me now. He had given the service an address.

12

THE HOUSE WAS the last in a row of ten that lined a short dead-end street a mile off the Belt Parkway at the edge of Jamaica Bay. There were no other streets near. The houses, all frame and old, were set like a single island in the bare salt marsh and bulrushes.

Jamaica Bay stretched bleak and frozen in the darkening afternoon as I parked the rental car in front of the isolated house. In the distance there were a few shacks on stilts, and a shiny new tract development that looked like an outpost in the desolate landscape of the moon. I was glad I had come alone, as instructed. No one could have approached the house unseen.

I went up the cleared path to the house and knocked. After a time the door was opened by an old man. He smoked a pipe.

"Can I help you, young man?" he said in a shaky voice.

"I'm looking for Mr. Weiss."

"Weiss? An old fellow? Tall and thin?"

"Short, fat and forty-odd. He sent for me. I'm alone."

The old man dropped the act. "Inside."

I went into a dim hallway, and a young man appeared with a gun. He frisked me. He led me through the house into a kitchen. An old woman sat at the kitchen table. My escort nodded to her that I was okay, and she waved him out. She looked motherly. Her gnarled hand gripped the neck of a bottle of straight rye. She had two cold brown eyes.

"I don't like visitors. I run a safe place. Seventeen years and no cop knows me."

"You must come expensive."

"No drunks, no hopheads, no women. In once and out once. No one comes back for a year if he's hot."

"And most of your guests are hot?"

"Flaming. They pay me to be safe. You're here because Weiss paid high. When you leave, you never heard of the place. I've got friends."

"Where's Sammy?"

"Second floor rear. You'll be watched, inside and out."

As I went up, I thought about the old woman. She probably made a fortune. Every day of the year she sat in this house getting rich and stewed. She wouldn't dare leave the place unwatched. She risked prison every day and slept with one eye open for money she would never spend because there was nothing she really wanted. Only the money.

Weiss opened the door to my knock. I felt like Stanley meeting Livingstone. He wore the same tie with the same stickpin. He hadn't been out of his clothes since Monday. He tried to give me a tough sneer—the big man.

"So now you come? You must of heard I got a roll."

"I've got a paying client," I said.

He smelled of fear. From the look of the room he had been lying on the bed sweating ever since he had arrived here.

"What client?" he croaked.

"Agnes Moore."

"Never heard of her. She in the Radford thing?"

"She is, and so are you."

He grabbed my sleeve. "I'm not, Danny! I hit the guy! How could I kill a guy with one punch?"

"He was knifed, Sammy. Stabbed."

He had my sleeve in both hands. "Knife? What knife? Paul never said nothing about no knife."

I watched him. "This place comes high, Sammy."

He sat down on the bed. "Five hundred a day, but it's safe, and tomorrow I get out, right? You're gonna help, right?"

"Did Paul Baron give you the money, Sammy?"

He grinned. "Paul don't give it to me, he made a good bet." He beamed at me. "It's a sign, you know? My luck's changed."

"A bet? What kind of bet?"

"With Cassel," he said. Cassel was a big horse-room owner. "The Baron laid the thousand he owed me for going up to Radford. A 25-1 shot at Caliente, and it came in!"

I suppose I stared. "Baron gave you $25,000? Cash?"

His dark eyes looked everywhere except at me. "It's my break, the sign. I'm okay now."

He knew it was all wrong, but he didn't want to know. We all dream of our rainbow. The gambler and petty crook can't wait for the dream to be real. They want it now, today, without the wait of working. They are hungry, and they are never bright, and they will believe that almost any impossibility will work out fine. They are sure the most stupid robbery will succeed, the slowest horse will win, the most impossible stroke of fortune will happen for them. Weiss had lived his life against the odds, and he had to believe a long-shot had come home for him. If Baron had tried to give him $25,000 he would have been suspicious. A bet that won on an inside tip was about the only way Baron could have gotten him to take the money. But a pretty sure way.

"Tell me the whole story now, Sammy," I said. "From the start. How did he happen to send you for the money at all?"

"I know The Baron a while, you know? I hang around. So he calls me Monday at the steam baths. Around noon; I always takes the steam before lunch, good for the blood. He says go up to Radford after one o'clock and collect. There's a grand in it for me. A thousand bucks, you know? So I goes, and then it all busts loose like I told you. That Radford was nuts."

"All right, now what happened after you left me?"

"I run into Misty at the corner. She told me Baron knew I was in a fix and he'd take care of me. She said to move around, but keep in touch, until Baron had a safe place to hide me."

"Baron could have contacted you at any time?"

"Sure. I called him every hour that night. He sent Leo Zar to pick me up about three-fifteen A.M. Leo's Baron's muscle-man."

"Did you know then that Radford was dead?"

"No, I swear. I'd been ducking Freedman too hard."

"Okay, go on."

Sammy wiped his face. "Leo took me to a dump up on 115th Street. I laid low all next day. Leo come up that night with a bottle and told me the guy was dead. He said Baron was short, but he had a hot tip and was gonna bet for me. Wednesday Leo moved me over to Brooklyn. About one A.M. Leo shows up again and tells me the horse come in! We sneaked over to Baron's pad. Baron paid me $25,000 and told me he'd got me in out here, and with all that dough he could get me out to Mexico. We go out for Mexico tomorrow, right?"

"We?" I said.

"You're gonna help, right? The Baron told me to get in touch with you."

"Baron told you to contact me? When? How?"

"A couple of hours ago. He sent a message out here."

I just watched him for a time. Maybe a minute. A minute of silence is an eternity. Weiss fidgeted, twisted, sweated. I let him sweat. I was going to hit him as hard as I could.

"You know that bet was a lie," I said. "You know that the money is exactly what Radford was supposed to have, and it's missing, Sammy. It's a frame-up! Baron told everyone you got the $25,000 and held out on him. He told the police that. The knife Radford was killed with is missing. You've got the money; you'll get the knife next! You're not going to Mexico; you're going to be found with the money and the knife. You'll probably be found dead."

"No!" His eyes were glazed with terror.

"Damn it, Baron killed Radford! That's where he got the $25,000. But you'll take the fall. Your only chance is to come with me, find Baron, and take him and your story to the police. It wasn't a gambling debt, Sammy; it was blackmail! They'll listen."

His fat quivered. "Get out! Get out!"

I don't know if I could have talked him out of his hole, out of the hope of all weak men that everything will blow over as long as they do nothing. But I didn't have to. The old woman and her gunman appeared at the door. The gunman had his gun.

"Out," the old woman snapped.

I should have known the room would be bugged.

"A frame-up is trouble," the old witch said. "I got no room for guys who think they're innocent. Out, both of you, fast!"

I thought for a moment that Weiss was going to faint. He didn't. I think he was afraid that if he passed out, he might never wake up. He stumbled for the door. I went behind him. We were herded down the stairs. The old man held the front door open. An icy blast greeted us. The woman gave us a parting message:

"One word and you're both dead! Don't come back."

The door closed. It was dark now, and the wind off the bay chewed at our faces. Weiss walked like a drunk. I got him into the car. I remembered the money.

"Where's the money, Sammy?"

He patted his suit coat. He had it in the lining.

"Okay," I said, trying to sound confident. "Let's get Baron."

13

I PARKED IN FRONT of my office and herded Weiss up. I called Mort Fenner at Cassel's horse room. I asked Mort to check on any bets made by Paul Baron on Wednesday that came in at 25-1. Mort didn't have to check. No 25-1 shot had come in all week.

"All you had to do was check the results," I said to Weiss.

Weiss said nothing. He had been too busy to check. He had been too scared. He might have learned the truth.

"Baron lives on East Sixteenth Street?" I said.

"He got a couple of pads," Weiss said reluctantly. "He paid me at the Fifth Street place, above the club."

I took my ancient .45 caliber service revolver out of the file. There is an exception to every rule. I hate the touch of a gun, it feels degrading, but there was a chance I was going to meet Paul Baron's gunman, Leo Zar, again, and the old cannon would stop a buffalo if I got close enough to hit.

When we reached Fifth Street, the club was doing business. The apartment entrance next to it was dark. Sammy pointed to a bell with no identification. I did not want to give Paul Baron that much warning. The inner door was old and had play on the buzzer-lock. I leaned on the door and gave a sharp kick. The lock sprung. I sent Weiss up ahead of me. He stepped as lightly as a cloud. Clear and present danger takes precedence over unfocused fear.

On the third floor I listened at the rear apartment door. I heard nothing. The lock was a common spring type, but picking is slow work. The door and frame were old and warped. I drew my cannon, motioned Weiss back against the corridor wall, and aimed my left foot for a hard kick just below the lock.

The door crashed open, and I jumped inside with my gun ready. You can feel emptiness. There was no one home. I put on the overhead light and called Weiss in. He came with those big eyes rolling in his sweating face. He stood in the exact center of the room as if he were afraid to be touched by anything.

"You're sure this is the place?" I asked him. Because the room was a surprise—it was a warm, comfortable room. The furniture was old, but it had been carefully cared-for as if by a woman.

"Sure I'm sure, Danny. We had a drink at that table."

"Did Baron live here with a woman?"

"There was a girl here when he paid me."

"Misty Dawn?"

"Nah, a young kid. Carla he called her."

Carla Devine, Paul Baron's other alibi witness. I felt even better. Then I went into the bedroom and switched on the light and didn't feel good anymore.

Paul Baron was on his back on the floor. The blood around him was brown and dry. There were two holes in his shirt. He seemed flat, and his flesh had shrunk into a leering grimace and a quarter-inch growth of beard. His left arm was flung out, and his right arm was twisted under his back in a position that would have been agony if he had been alive. I rolled him over gingerly. He was stiff as steel and moved all in a piece. The hand under his back held a wicked five-inch switchblade. He had not gone gentle, but he had gone. I let the body fall back and looked under the bed.

In the living room there was a strangled groan, and feet running, stumbling away.

I ran out into the living room. Weiss was clawing at the broken door. I reached him just as he got it open. I got a neck-hold on him and dragged him back. We went down, and I lost my grip. I cursed my missing arm. Sammy crawled to his feet. I made it up and jumped to block the door. I've never seen a cornered animal, but now I know what one looks like. He came at me like a man turned into a rhinoceros. I hauled out my heavy revolver.

"Stop it, Sammy!"

Weiss couldn't hear, or didn't want to, and deep down in his cunning little brain he knew I wouldn't shoot. He came at me with both hands flailing. I swung the gun and got him on the shoulder. He grunted. I slashed at him again and got his left hand. It must have jammed his thumb. He howled and sat down on the floor and sucked at his thumb like a giant baby. The deep Levantine eyes looked up at me with unbelieving sorrow: I was ruining him, killing him.

"You wouldn't last two hours, Sammy," I said as gently as I could. "I'm the only friend you've got now."

"Some friend! Some friend!" His voice was like a hurt child.

I squatted and looked into his face. "Listen to me, Sammy. Baron is dead. He set you up for a frame on the Radford murder, and now he can't be made to admit it and clear you. I think he killed Radford himself, but maybe I'll never prove it now."

He listened, but I'm not sure he heard. His face was that of an animal caught in a forest fire, and there was only one thing on his mind: escape. Run, run, even if it was into a river or over a cliff. But I had to reach him.

"Tell me exactly what happened here last night, Sammy."

He blinked, thought, and the effort seemed to bring him out of his trance a little. "I told you, Danny. I came up, we had a drink, he gave me my money, and I went out to that hideout."

"Who drove you out? Leo Zar?"

"Leo wasn't here; he never come up. I grabbed a cab out front. There's a stand outside the club."

"You took a taxi all the way out to Jamaica Bay?"

"Sure, why not? I had the dough."

I sighed. "Anyone else see you go in or come out?"

"A drunk was giving one of the tenants a hard time in the front hall when I come out."

I just looked at him. He was all the way out of his panic now. In a way I wished he wasn't. It would hurt more.

"Baron's been dead around twenty-four hours, Sammy. Since just about when you were here last night. Did you kill him, Sammy? Did you spot the frame? Did he try to hold you to turn you in? Did you know he killed Radford, so he tried to kill you to shut you up before he called the cops and handed them a dead fugitive?"

He scrambled up. "I didn't kill no one! I never had no gun my whole life. I can't hardly shoot a gun."

It was impossible to tell if he was lying or not. Fear was deep in Weiss, but so was cunning. If he had killed both Radford and Baron, he would have talked and acted the same way.

"No one will believe the bet, Sammy," I said. "No one could, and there was no bet. They'll believe you got the money from Radford or from Baron, they won't care which. You killed Radford for the money, or Baron killed him for the money. They won't care about that, either. They'll be sure one of you killed Radford, and they'll close the books, because Baron's dead and they'll nail you for his killing."

He shrank away. "No, I swear!"

"You were seen leaving here just about when Baron died. A cab driver gets one call a year that takes him to a place like Jamaica Bay, so he'll remember you good. Everyone knows Baron was looking for you. You have the money. I'll give **you** odds no one saw Baron alive after you left, if he was."

Sammy stared at me, and suddenly there were tears in his cow eyes. Big, hopeless tears like a crying hippo, only it wasn't funny. I was thinking of what I could say to help him, when a great, wide smile spread over his face among the tears as suddenly as the tears themselves had started.

"The girl! Carla! She was here when I left! It's okay, it's okay, Danny. Find that girl. Carla. She'll tell you."

I watched him. He had mentioned the girl earlier, so maybe it was true. Maybe the sun was going to shine on Sammy at last.

"All right. We'll find the girl. I think I know where to find her. You can describe her first to Gazzo to show him you really saw her."

"Gazzo?" His smile faded. "You got to hide me!"

"No, Sammy." I held the gun. "No more running. If you're not lying in your teeth, there's a killer around who's framing you six ways from Sunday. Baron figures as Radford's killer, but someone killed Baron. If you were found good and dead, maybe a suicide, that would tie it all up neat and end the case for the cops. On the loose you're a clay pigeon."

"I don't care! I'm not . . ."

"Yes you are. For both of us. Just by being here I'm harboring a fugitive, concealing a felony, and obstructing the law. If you're innocent, I hope I can prove it for you. If you're guilty, I'm not taking the fall with you."

"Some pal! You don't believe me. I'm going!"

He moved. I let off the safety. He stopped.

"I'll shoot, Sammy. You're a fugitive, and you've been a liar all your life. I'll put you in the hospital if I have to."

He looked at the gun. His face was like raw putty. I put the gun down where I could reach it fast, and called Gazzo.

Weiss shivered alone in the center of the room.

14

IT WAS PAST 3:00 A.M. when I followed Gazzo into his office. He was just barely talking to me. He did not like the way I had taken Weiss to find Baron, and he did not like it that I had gone to find Weiss on my own in the first place.

"You going to bust that hideout?" I asked.

"Afraid for your skin?"

"You bet I am."

"For now we'll just keep an eye on the place."

He sat behind his desk and stared at me. I sat and stared back. Weiss had stuck to his story through two shifts of questions. I did not know how long he could go on, even if it were all true. Weiss still insisted he had only scuffled with Radford even when they showed him the pictures of the body. He had tried to look away. Death scared him. They made him look, but all he did was stare and say that the guy had been okay when he had run.

I said, "I figure Baron went in the back way after Sammy ran. He got rough, or Radford did, and Radford got killed. Baron grabbed the money. Then he got scared. Sammy was the perfect pigeon. Baron laid the frame on him, or tried to. That's all that explains Baron's actions."

"Maybe," Gazzo said, "if you believe Weiss. If you believe Baron, it plays different. Weiss killed Radford, took the money, and ran. Baron went looking for him. Baron found him. Baron got tough, and Weiss killed him."

"Sammy killed a man like Baron? With Leo Zar around?"

"A cornered rat," Gazzo said. "Anyway, Weiss has the money now. It doesn't matter if Weiss had the money all along, or if Baron did.

Baron didn't give the money to Weiss, not Paul Baron. That bet story is really great."

There it was. Either Weiss killed both of them, or only Paul Baron. The police could see it no other way, and they'd settle for charging Weiss with Baron's murder alone. They could be right. Weiss was a born liar. Only the bet story was so bad I believed it.

"How do you know the money was Radford's money?"

"He had a list of the serial numbers in his desk."

"So that's why you wanted to know if Weiss had paid me?"

"That's right." Gazzo studied his ceiling. "Baron was shot from close with a .45 caliber automatic. The first shot knocked him flat. The second hit him when he was down. The first was still in him. The M.E. can't place the time any better than between eleven P.M. and five A.M. Wednesday night. But Baron was talking to me until one A.M. that night, so it was after that."

"He was giving you his story about looking for Weiss."

"I don't know that he wasn't," Gazzo said. "Weiss admits he got to Baron around one-thirty A.M. He says he left around two-thirty. The taxi driver remembers the long haul out to Jamaica Bay, and the super at the place remembers Weiss because of the drunk he was battling when Weiss passed him going out. No one saw Baron alive again."

"Except maybe the girl."

"We're bringing her in now. I hope she can clear Weiss."

"What about the shots? Anyone hear them?"

"It was the Village, Dan. Ten people heard something like shots, ranging between nine and four A.M. Who knows?"

"What about the knife and the gun?"

"Don't fence with me, Dan. Those weapons are in the river, or in Jamaica Bay. We'll never find them unless Weiss tells us where he threw them."

"I don't like a frame that turns into a real murder."

"If the first killing is a frame," Gazzo said. "Let's say it is. Okay, that's just what I do like. It gives Weiss a double motive to kill Baron." He leaned across the desk. "Look, Dan, if Weiss didn't kill Baron, you're stuck with only two other explanations, both beauties. Maybe it was two frame-ups of the same man by two different parties, which is some coincidence to hand the D.A. Or maybe Baron worked out a double frame-up that hinged on himself getting killed! Now there's a theory."

I said nothing. What could I say? I was sure Baron had been trying to frame Weiss for Radford's murder. Only now Weiss was on the hook for Baron's killing, and it didn't figure that a man would frame someone for his own murder! The D.A. would have a field day with that. The way it was now, the more I proved that Baron had been framing Weiss for Radford, the worse it was going to look for Weiss as Baron's killer.

Gazzo was watching me squirm mentally, when his pretty sergeant came in to announce that Carla Devine was outside.

"Send her in," Gazzo said.

She came in slow, taking a little two-step as if pushed. She was a lovely little creature: small, dark, with ivory skin, a madonna face, and eyes as big as a dark satin bed. The eyes were frightened. She held her handbag in both hands like a child holding a schoolbag.

"Sit down, Miss Devine," Gazzo said.

She perched. Her mini-skirt left little unseen. She had young, hard, fresh legs. I looked. Gazzo didn't. That seemed to scare her more. Men usually stared at her legs.

"Tell me where you were Wednesday night, Miss Devine?"

"Wednesday?" She watched Gazzo's face. "Gee, I think I was with Paul."

"Paul Baron?" Dark lines grooved between Gazzo's eyes. He was surprised. So was I. I was also hopeful.

"We went to dinner. Sure, that was Wednesday," she said.

"And after dinner?" Gazzo said.

"He took me home. He had to go somewhere."

"Where is home?"

"University Place. Number 47, apartment 12-C."

"What time did he take you home?"

"Maybe ten-thirty. He had to go somewhere by eleven."

"He went to see me," Gazzo said. "He left here about one A.M. Where did he pick you up after that?"

She fluttered her lashes. "You mean that same night? He didn't pick me up again. He hasn't been around since he took me home Wednesday. Paul's like that. He comes, he goes."

"You didn't see Baron after ten-thirty Wednesday night?" Gazzo said. "You're sure? We'll find out, Miss Devine."

"I didn't, honest. Has . . . has Paul done something?"

I leaned toward her. "You were with Baron in his Fifth Street apartment at one-thirty Wednesday night. You saw Baron pay off a man named Weiss for a bet."

She gave me her big brown eyes. "You mean Sammy Weiss? Gee, that wasn't Wednesday night. That was maybe a week ago. I don't go to that Fifth Street place much. Misty lives there. I saw Sammy Weiss there a week ago, maybe; only there wasn't no bet."

It was hard to believe that she was lying. Gazzo wouldn't believe it. He would believe that Weiss was lying.

Carla Devine said, "Is Paul in trouble?"

I said, "Baron said he was with you Monday afternoon. Was he?"

"Sure, he came . . ."

"Baron's dead," I said. "He doesn't need an alibi now."

"Dead?"

Gazzo snapped, "Was he with you Monday afternoon?"

She nodded. "Yes, but . . . not when I said. He came about two-thirty, not one-thirty. He told me to say one-thirty. Dead? He's dead?"

Her knuckles whitened on her bag, and she slipped off the chair in a dead faint. Gazzo jumped as if bitten. If it was an act, it was good. Gazzo bawled for his female sergeant.

"Take care of her. When she comes around, get a statement."

The sergeant got some help, and they carried Carla Devine out. I watched her go. She was taking Weiss's chances with her.

"He's lying all the way, Dan," Gazzo said.

"The girl lied before."

"For Baron. Maybe Baron did kill Radford after all, but he's dead. Why would she lie now?"

Gazzo said it almost bitterly. A good detective like Gazzo works close to danger. He works even closer to something else—the edge of sanity that yawns like an abyss for men who must decide, in essence, who lives and who dies. Gazzo is not a pitiless man, and that makes it hard for him to have to decide what a piece of human debris like Weiss is, or is not, guilty of doing. That gives a man scars inside, makes him bitter.

We both sat silent for a time. Then I said:

"How did Radford happen to have a list of the bills?"

"Who knows? Maybe he always did it when he had a lot of cash around, or maybe it was a trap for Baron. You tell me it was a blackmail con, not a bet. Maybe Radford was being cute."

We sat in another silence. I couldn't think of anything else to ask, or to object to. After a while I got up and put on my duffle coat. Gazzo watched me.

"Weiss is guilty, Dan. Let it go."

"Maybe," I said. "I'd like to find those weapons, you know? Stir the water. That's detective work, right?"

"Damn you," Gazzo said.

He would work on it, as I would, but maybe he'd never know for sure. Only the D.A. would be sure. The D.A. had to be elected, and he would tell himself that he was sure.

I went down to the street and got into my car. It was bitter cold. I sat and watched the Annex entrance. I smoked too many cigarettes.

It was nearly dawn before Carla Devine came out. Gazzo was an honest cop; he had sweated her hard. She had not changed her story. If she had, she would not have been coming out.

She hurried along the iron-cold street away from me. I got out and followed. She was huddled in a fur coat like something that had forgotten to hibernate. The door of a battered gray coupe swung open in front of her. I ran. She saw me, and jumped into the car. I got my hand on the door handle. The coupe ground gears and pulled away, dragging me. Her great brown eyes stared up into my face from inside. A thin, pale, wild-haired young boy was behind the wheel, his lips skinned back from his teeth.

One thing a one-armed man can't do is get the door of a moving car open, or hang on when the car gets above 20 m.p.h. The speed turned me around backwards. I had to let go, and landed hard on my back in the street. I didn't bother to see where the car had gone. I wasn't going to get the number in the dark.

After a time I got up. I drove the rental car home. I went to bed. What could I have gotten from Carla Devine anyway?

15

SOMEONE WAS CRYING. I stumbled naked through the snow and saw that it was my arm huddled behind a garbage can. Then it wasn't my arm crying, it was Sammy Weiss. Three big men appeared and began to pound the lids of the garbage cans into Sammy's face. I began to moan. Then my father was clutching at my empty sleeve, and I was telling him to get lost, get lost, get lost. . . .

I woke with sun in my eyes, and knew that it was Weiss who I wanted to get lost, go away, vanish.

I lighted a cigarette. I lay in bed feeling empty. I was at a dead end, literally. I had worked hard on the vague hunch that Weiss had not killed Jonathan Radford. I had just about been sure that Paul Baron had killed the man. Now Baron was dead, and the case against Weiss was stronger than ever.

Was he lying? I didn't know. All I knew was that if I had killed two men, I'd lie all the way.

I got up and plugged in the coffee. I turned on my heaters. I sat at the kitchen table. All right, I was at a dead end because there were too many variables, too many possibilities. Science has a method of tackling problems with too many variables and not enough facts. Scientists assume certain variables to be fixed, and then make an hypothesis to explain the facts they do know. The hypothesis may not be true, but it gives them a start.

I waited until the coffee was ready, and poured a cup. My assumption, my fixed variable, was that Weiss was telling the truth. My hypothesis was that Paul Baron had killed Jonathan Radford. It might not be true, but it fitted the facts enough to be workable, and it gave me a simple line of reasoning to follow: why had Baron been killed?

Radford is dead. Then what? Revenge? The family would have let the law handle Baron if they knew he had killed Jonathan. My client, Agnes Moore? She had a reason, and probably the hate and the courage. It was possible. I could work on that.

Radford is dead. Baron starts to frame Weiss. The frame seems to work well, the cops go howling after Weiss. Baron still has the material to blackmail Walter Radford. Did he try to use it again, go on with the squeeze with Walter now rich? Or did someone just think he might try to go on, and move to stop him? Remove the threat once and for all?

Or had some associate of Baron's, some friend, become scared after Radford's murder and decided that Baron was too dangerous to have around? Someone who was involved with Baron and no longer trusted Baron after Radford's murder?

Or maybe some associate of Baron's had decided to keep the blackmail all to himself. A partner who got greedy.

Partner?

Another rule of science says look at the facts, no matter how ridiculous they seem. No man would frame another man for his own murder. But that was exactly what Baron had done. Two facts that could not both be true, and yet were. One answer: Baron had not known what he was really doing. He had been manipulated.

Someone had changed the plan, had fooled Baron into framing Weiss for Baron's own murder. Someone close enough to Baron, and to the whole scheme, to know everything that Baron did, and even to control much of what Baron did. A person who must have been working with Baron all along. An unknown partner.

The proof was staring at me: the message Baron had sent to Weiss to contact me. Weiss hadn't questioned the message because as far as he knew only Baron knew where he was. But Baron had been long dead when that message was sent to Weiss.

I began to dress. Someone who knew that Baron was dead had sent the message. To flush Weiss out, to lead me to Weiss, and, eventually, to Baron. Once I heard Weiss's story, there were only two ways I could act: go and find Baron, as I had done; or turn Weiss in to the police. Then the police would find Baron. Once Baron was found, no one would believe Weiss's story. Everything would point to Weiss as Baron's killer. Mission accomplished.

I went out to the nearest Riker's for breakfast. Gazzo would say that there had been no message, that Weiss had cooked up the story to convince me that he didn't know Baron was dead. Gazzo could be right, but my assumption was that Weiss was not lying. That meant there was a partner. Leo Zar had known where Weiss was, but Leo didn't fit my picture. He was too obvious, he would have had to work in a different way, and I didn't see him as a partner or double-dealer. He was a subordinate, a soldier for Baron, the loyal retainer. I could be wrong.

While I waited for my eggs, I called the Radford house in North Chester. The butler said that Walter was not home, but Mrs. Radford was. I waited and heard a click on the line. No one spoke. A moment later Mrs. Radford came on.

"You again, Mr. Fortune?" she said.

"Sorry. Can you tell me if everyone was up there Wednesday night, late? Between midnight and five A.M. Start with yourself."

"You're a direct man. I presume I was in bed. Has something more happened?"

"A man named Paul Baron was shot. Didn't the police call?"

"Why would they call? I told you I knew no Paul Baron."

"Walter knew him."

"Then I suppose they would call Walter."

"Was he at home Wednesday night?"

"No, he and Deirdre went to New York. They stayed the night with George, I believe."

"How about your daughter?"

"Morgana? Why, I think she was here. Yes, I'm sure."

"How sure?"

"Really, Mr. Fortune, you spoke to her yourself that evening. But, of course, she does have her own cottage. I don't watch her. That was the night before the funeral. We buried poor Jonathan yesterday. I'm sure she was here."

I thanked her and listened to her hang up. I waited. The line did not go dead at once. There was a brief pause before it clicked dead.

I went back to my eggs.

Walter Radford answered the door of the East Sixty-third Street apartment. His face was drawn, and his chip eyes were smaller than ever. His lip twitched, and his manners were down.

"What do you want?"

"Some more questions."

His smile seemed to hurt him. "Go away."

He tried to stare me down, but it wasn't his character. I stared back and pushed in past him. I detected changes already. There were two tall brass lamps with gaudy shades, a fustian armchair with footstool, and a carved smoking stand. The balance had been ruined. A bachelor Victorian gentleman fussiness had crept into the room. It looked like George Ames was out from under the hand of Jonathan.

I turned on Walter. "I know what the $25,000 was really about. So do the police, although I doubt if they'll do much about your lying, seeing who you are, and that they figure the case is solved."

"I don't know what you're talking about."

"Just how much did Baron have on you?"

"Baron had nothing on me. You can't prove he did."

"You mean with Baron dead it can't be proved? Lucky."

He clenched his fists, took a step toward me. I grinned. He had two hands, but I had seen him swing at Costa. It isn't often I feel in command of a physical situation. His hands dropped.

"Go away, Fortune. Please."

His voice was as plaintive as that of a small boy asking a domineering father to leave him alone.

"The way it stands you had the prime motive to kill Baron. If he murdered Jonathan, he'd have wanted money for a fast fade. Did he go on with the squeeze? Did he contact you?"

"Of course not! And I didn't know he was dead until the police called this morning. I lied about the blackmail, yes. Why admit I'd been involved in illegal business? I had no idea that Paul might have killed my uncle. I don't know that he did. The police seem to think that Weiss killed them both."

"And that suits you fine."

"I don't really care one way or the other."

"You're rich, and Baron is dead. End of the affair?"

"Why not?"

"Whoever killed Baron has what he had against you."

His lip twitched again, but he said nothing.

"Was one of Baron's witnesses Carla Devine?"

"Yes. The little bitch was in love with Paul."

"Who else? Misty Dawn?"

"No one else, not as a partner, if that's what you mean. He had names, places, checks, photographs."

"Tell me how he worked it."

"We played poker and I lost. Not $25,000; about $5,000. He was nice about it, but he said he really needed the money. I told him I couldn't get any more from Jonathan. He said he understood, but he was in trouble and couldn't wait. He said he had an idea of how I could pay it off fast. There were some girls he worked with who would pay for contacts. I had plenty of rich friends. If I arranged dates, the girls would pay me, and so would the men if I worked it right. I liked the idea. I'd use my sacred family position to make money. So I contacted old friends and acquaintances, especially those in companies who entertained out-of-town customers. Everyone was happy. I made money. Then Paul lowered the trap."

"When was all this? A timetable."

"I met Paul about seven months ago as I told you. I started with the girls about three months ago. Paul revealed his dirty scheme last Sunday."

"And sent Weiss to collect on Monday? He must have called Jonathan first to show his hand and put on the pressure, and he told Weiss it was only a gambling debt."

"I don't know what he did. I thought he was waiting."

"So the blackmail was really on Jonathan, for the family. He had to move while his evidence was hot."

"I told him Jonathan would not pay!"

"He should have listened to you," I said dryly. "Now tell me where you were on Wednesday night. All night."

He glared at me. He seemed like a man writhing in a net. Not scared or nervous, but desperate, unhappy.

"Why should I?"

"Because I'll hound you until I find out."

"Oh, very well. I had tickets for the theater. I'd had them for weeks. I didn't think we should go the night before the funeral, but Mother said why not? Deirdre agreed. I have the theater stubs, I can describe the show. We stopped for drinks at Downey's. We know the waiter. We had some supper and came straight home here. George was here. We all went out for the funeral in the morning."

"What time did you get home here?"

"About two o'clock."

George Ames picked that moment to make his entrance. He must have been waiting in the wings. He swept into the room in an impeccable gray tweed suit with a wide black band on the sleeve. A tweed coat was draped over his shoulders, the arms hanging free.

"You are a busy man, Mr. Fortune. I once played Sherlock Holmes and barely moved from a chair all night."

"Different times, different methods," I said. "What time did you get home on Wednesday night, Mr. Ames?"

"Wednesday? Let me see, that was the night I talked to you out in North Chester, correct?"

"That was the night."

"Yes. I came home early that night. It had been a strain with the family. I'd say I arrived here about midnight. I needed rest for the funeral."

"So from two A.M. on only you two and Deirdre Fallon were here to alibi each other?"

"Are you implying a family conspiracy?" Ames snapped.

"Baron was a con man squeezing the clan," I said. "You would all have considered him vermin to be expunged."

"Then I suggest you prove that one of us was elsewhere."

"There are other members of the family. You could have hired Baron killed."

"You have much to work on."

"Did you introduce Jonathan to Agnes Moore?"

"So you are a detective. Your appearance makes people underestimate you, doesn't it?" Ames said, studying me. "Yes, I failed to strike a chord in Agnes, but she liked Jonathan instantly. She and I did a TV special on old-style burlesque. I did a music hall routine. Not my forte, really, but I rather enjoyed . . ."

I heard reminiscences coming. "You knew he was seeing her?"

"I surmised he was, yes."

"Who else knew or surmised?"

"No one, I should think. He kept his private needs quiet, as we all do, don't we?" He began to draw on a pair of gray gloves. "I enjoy talking to you, Mr. Fortune, but I'm late for the club. Routine is the opium of the elegant aged. Walter?"

Walter was at a window looking out. He was looking at the city below, but I guessed that what he saw was inside his head. His hands at his sides were clenched into fists again.

"Walter?" Ames repeated. "Shall I see you for dinner?"

"What?" Walter turned. "Oh, I don't know. I . . . it depends on what Deirdre wants to do."

"Let me know, will you?" Ames said. He inclined his head to me, and strode from the room. It was a good exit. Ames was always onstage, and I wondered about him. Maybe he had needed some fast money and had learned about Walter's sideline.

I said to Walter, "Can I talk to Miss Fallon?"

"She's out." He was back at his window. "Go away, Fortune."

"Sure," I said, "but I just had a funny idea. What if the blackmail was only a cover? You cooked it up with Baron to have your uncle murdered, and then got rid of Baron. Tricky, eh? But I can't get it out of my mind that you seem to gain most from both murders."

He turned. "When I got my money within a year anyway?"

"Yeh, that's the stumbling block, but I'll work on it. Of course, maybe it was to get the company. That you wouldn't have inherited until Jonathan was dead."

"The company? I didn't want the company. I still don't."

"Somebody could have wanted it for you. They're pushing you."

"You're insane! Crazy!"

I said, "Or maybe the blackmail was legitimate. Just for kicks. You helped Baron work it to watch Uncle steam, and to make a fast buck. You thought it was fun to work with those girls. But it got out of hand, Uncle got killed, and you had to cover by erasing Baron. Now that's not bad. I like that."

He stared at me and chewed his lip. I gave him a grin and walked out. My guessing at him had been pure fantasy, but it was all possible, and if there was a grain of truth in it anywhere, I might worry him into some move. That was the idea, anyway.

He looked worried enough when I left.

16

NUMBER 47 University Place turned out to be where Deirdre Fallon had sent me to look for Paul Baron on Tuesday night. In the daylight it was a gray building without style or character. The typical New York apartment house—no taste, only floor space. I went up to 12-C. It was the same apartment I had been to on Tuesday. This time I got an answer.

An older woman who looked like a cleaning woman, and held a dust mop to prove it, opened the door. I asked for Carla Devine. She told me to wait, she'd go ask the girls. I waited.

The large room was rich and bright, with a deep-pile yellow carpet. Everything was expensive, thick and pastel-colored. You could have seen a speck of ash for a mile. It was all arranged in separate furniture groupings like a series of private waiting rooms. There were even magazines on the coffee tables.

It was the kind of apartment where a group of girls band together to live better than most men could ever keep them. That is a way of life in New York. Most of the girls are from out of town and have ambitions. They are office workers, subprofessionals, or fringe artists serving commerce, and what they really want is "fun" and, eventually, a man who makes more money than their fathers did.

Some of these girls change along the way, usually the most beautiful. Their work becomes a token, the men they meet have a great deal more money than Dad, their fun becomes expensive fun, and they begin to make a little profit on the fun. They have to be taken to the Colony for a hamburger. When they ask for money for the ladies' room, they expect ten dollars and give no change. For this they render a reward, and that moves them across the shadow line between amateurs and at least semi-pros.

I was sure that these were the girls Walter Radford had worked with, and I was thinking about Walter and his rich friends, when an inner door opened and Deirdre Fallon came into the room.

"You again, Mr. Fortune," she said.

She wore a black suit, a high-necked black sweater, and a smile. The suit showed her off better than even the white dress had. She walked toward me. She wore black knee boots that did things to my backbone. Her eyes were amused. I suppose I had the look of a man slapped in the face with a flounder. We all think in stereotypes.

"Maybe you're following me," I said.

"No, this happens to be where I live. Or it's where I lived until Walter's mother invited me out to North Chester. You'd have learned sooner or later in your wanderings."

"You live here?" I was asking about more than her address, and she knew it. Her smile became wider. I really amused her.

"How do you think I met Walter? A man with your experience shouldn't jump to conclusions on so little evidence. This isn't 1900; the world is a lot more fluid."

"It's not 1900," I agreed. "You met Walter when he started to work with the girls here?"

"No, earlier. Paul Baron brought him to a party soon after they met. Six months ago. We liked each other."

She thought about it, and frowned at her thoughts. She sat down on a pink couch and held her hand out. "Do you have a cigarette?"

I gave her a cigarette and lighted it. She went on with her silent thinking. Outside the high windows heavy clouds were moving in a blanket across the sun from the north. I could hear the wind shake the windows. She smoked like a man, slow and steady.

"Genteel poverty," she said. "The very common story of my first sixteen years. The proud and proper Presbyterian Irish. If you want to observe false pride on its narrowest level, have a good look at a minority within a minority. My father was prejudiced against everyone who wasn't Irish, everyone who was Irish if also Catholic, and everyone who mistook him for a Catholic Irishman. The only group he didn't feel superior to was the English aristocracy, and he wasn't always sure about them. He had a high opinion of himself, my mother was delicately well-bred, and I got a fine polish with the aid of richer friends. With it all, we didn't have a penny to put on the eyes of the dead."

"It's not a new problem," I said.

"As old as time. My father died, my mother went to Baltimore as a poor relation, and I went out into the big world. I had culture, style, and good grammar. I was straight out of *Jane Eyre*. The little lady without money, connections, or salable skills. Only I wasn't Jane Eyre, the world had changed, and the little lady had changed with it. I got work right out in public because I'm damned good-looking and there's a market for front these days. I didn't have to be a governess in a big house with a brooding master I dreamed of marrying. I could be myself."

Her laugh was warm if not exactly genteel. "Men liked me. I'm the cool type, right? Austere and untouched. That appealed to many men, especially rich older men. I wanted what I wanted. I took it the way I could get it. I enjoyed my life. What did I have to do that I didn't want to do, that most girls don't do today? The only essential difference was that I confined my social life to rich men who could move me in rich circles, and that I didn't pretend that they loved me or that I loved them. In a way I think we're more honest here. All girls get wined, dined, and given gifts by men they don't really give a damn about; they only tell themselves they do to feel chaste. Some of what men gave me bought clothes and paid the rent, yes, but that isn't so unusual these days either. I may not have loved any of them, but I never went with a man I didn't like. I never had to; maybe I was lucky." She stopped and seemed to be thinking about her luck. It didn't appear to make her ecstatic.

"Why tell me?" I said. "I was never ordained."

"All men are ordained on that subject," she said. "But I'm not apologizing. It's over now, but I enjoyed the last four years. No regrets. You're forming theories, and I want you to form the right theories.

Walter seems to love me. I don't love him in the normal sense, but I've never needed love. I like him, and I like to be loved. I think I can do him good. I intend to try."

"Especially now that he's really rich."

"That won't hurt. I like what money can buy, and that's most of everything. Perhaps that's what I've been telling you. But he asked me to marry him some time ago, and Jonathan liked me."

"I wouldn't know," I said. "Were you part of the squeeze?"

"I'd hardly have been worth Paul Baron's time."

"You would be worth a lot to Walter. Or maybe Jonathan wouldn't have liked you if he had known about the last four years."

She smoothed her skirt over her lap. "I may have been part of Baron's pressure, yes. But not seriously. Walter knows all about me. So does Mrs. Radford, and so did Jonathan. Even George Ames knows. I told you I had no apologies. I learned that you can't live with a false front, why should you? I don't need Walter so much I would hide myself. As it happens, Mrs. Radford seems to admire me for it all, and so did Jonathan. They seemed to feel that I showed initiative and determination."

I could believe it, from what I had seen of the Radfords. You didn't get rich a hundred years ago, or today, in a commercial society by being soft or particularly moral. To the old pirates of commerce, morality was relative. It still is.

"You knew Baron before you met Walter?"

"Of course. We were all invited to his parties to make contacts. He didn't introduce me to Walter, but I did meet Walter at that party. Are you thinking that one of us killed Paul Baron?"

"Who's us? The girls here, or the Radford clan?"

"Either."

"I don't know the girls, but Baron was trouble for the Radfords. I think he killed Jonathan, and that gives the family two first-rate motives."

"Revenge? Hardly," she said, "and if one of them was going to kill Paul Baron, why not do it before he got to Jonathan?"

"Maybe Jonathan tried to do it. And then, after Jonathan was dead, Baron tried to go on with the blackmail."

She gave me a cool frown, but said nothing.

"Tell me about Carla Devine," I said.

"I can't tell you much. She's relatively new here. She was Paul Baron's latest conquest. He tried us all at one time or another. He dazzled Carla."

"Did he try you?"

"Naturally. He didn't dazzle me."

"Is Carla here?"

"She didn't come home last night, the girls tell me. She's done that before, but she was usually with Paul Baron then."

"Do you know a friend of hers, a boy with an old, gray coupe? Thin, pale, long wild hair."

"No. No one like that comes here."

"Do you know where she might have gone?"

She seemed to think. "She talked about her parents at times. They live in a place called City Island. Mr. Gerald Devine; 42 Throggs Lane."

"All right, Miss Fallon, and thanks." I stood.

"You might as well make it Deirdre. We seem to be fated to meet often." She looked at my empty sleeve. Her eyes were foggy tunnels. "Someday you'll tell me about your arm."

"No I won't."

"The story is reserved for someone special?"

"Yes."

She nodded. "I'll walk out with you."

She went into the next room and came back wearing a perky fur hat on her chestnut hair. She carried a fur coat that had to be sable. She handed it to me. It felt like my income for two years, if I had good years. She didn't touch me as she slipped into the coat. She didn't have to. Just being that close, I felt her down to my shoes.

We went out and down in the elevator. She looked like a Russian princess—the rosy princess bundled in fur and boots a boy dreams about when he's fifteen and reading Tolstoy. She made me dream her naked. That was bad. It would have been bad even if I wasn't investigating a murder. She didn't fit with five rooms without central heat.

On the street she gave me her hand. "I think you're a tenacious man, Mr. Fortune. Be careful. I may try to make you tell me the story of your arm someday."

I smiled. It was all I could think to do. She walked to a small red Fiat. I watched the Fiat drive off. I think I waved.

17

CITY ISLAND is in the Bronx. It is near Orchard Beach—a strip of brown sand and shallow water where a million people wade on hot summer days like Hindus in the Ganges and feel privileged.

City Island itself is barely an island now, but they still build and berth boats up there. Not long ago it was a true haven from the grime of the city. Today it is just a part of the Bronx: a little less crowded, and with a few more trees.

Gerald Devine's house was squeezed among shabby wooden-box type houses and a dispirited red brick apartment building. It faced the sullen, scummy water of Long Island Sound. The land in front of the house at the edge of the water was all rock, but there was no grandeur. A sluggish tide lapped like oil at the black rocks. Leafless gray trees looked as alive as laundry poles.

In this bleak landscape where even the snow was gray, Devine's house shone like a miniature diamond. It was a small, white Cape Cod cottage set in a neat yard that must have been all flowers in summer. The picket fence around the yard was like well-capped teeth. I parked in the swept driveway behind a 1947 Packard Clipper that looked almost new.

The door of the house opened before I reached it. A stocky man with thin, fine gray hair and a pink complexion watched me approach. A crooked smile that had probably been considered roguish when he was young flirted with his thin mouth but didn't quite take. His blue eyes were small, clear, and questioning.

"Mr. Gerald Devine?" I asked.

"I am," he said. "Is it Carla you want?"

The lilt of Ireland was unmistakable in his voice. A soft accent, and at another time I might have enjoyed identifying the county. Not now.

"I'm not the first, Mr. Devine?"

"Third," he said. "No one comes after Carla anymore. We see little of her ourselves. Now three come in a morning. It's trouble, isn't it?"

"Tell me about the other two," I said.

He rubbed his upper lip. "I don't know. You better come in."

I followed him into a small, clean room cluttered with furniture as old as the Packard and just as well-tended. A woman sat in a reclining chair. She had dark, worried eyes. Her black hair showed no gray at all. She was small, dark, and still pretty. She was younger than Devine, but not that much younger. One of the Spanish Irish who never seem old until they suddenly become crones. There was no doubt that she was Carla's mother.

"Sit down, Mr. . . . ?" Devine said.

"Fortune," I said. "Dan Fortune."

He brightened. "Irish?"

"It was Fortunowski. My dad edited it for modern readers."

The woman's voice was a whisper. "Is . . . is Carla in bad trouble? Has she . . . done something?"

"No," I said. "I'm just trying to find her to ask some questions. It's a case I'm on."

"Case?" Devine said. "You're a policeman?"

"Private." I showed him my credentials.

The woman said, "She lives with some girls. On University Place. It's a fine apartment."

"Mr. Fortune knows that, dear," Devine said gently. He leaned toward me from where he sat on a stuffed settee. "The others didn't have any credentials. You said a case?"

"Your daughter might be a kind of witness, Mr. Devine. Do you know a man named Paul Baron?"

"No. We don't know anything Carla does in the city. What kind of case?"

"Murder," I said. "Maybe two murders. Blackmail, too."

The woman made a sound. Just a sound without a name. Devine clasped his hands between his knees. He looked up and at me, and past me out a window. He had a view of the greasy water, and maybe a scow or a mud flat.

"They have to grow up, you know?" Devine said. "A child, ah, that's a marvelous thing. Small, pretty, vulnerable and happy. No matter how they cry and you have to smack them, they're happy little things. They run and jump and swing and throw themselves into the snow. It's all so marvelous for them. I used to watch her and almost cry. They don't know, children. About life, death, all that. But they grow up and they find out how short it is, life, and they want their share. It has to be that way. I always understood. Carla wanted a lot of things I didn't want, her mother didn't want, so she had to go and find them. You can't give your child what you have, what you wanted. It's natural. I never expected her to stay here."

I said nothing. He wasn't finished. The woman watched him with those dark eyes as if this were something they had talked about a lot. They had understood, decided that Carla was right, that the risks where worth it for her to live. They were right, of course, but it's no easier to be right than wrong.

"I didn't want her to stay up here," Devine said. "When I bought the land back in 'thirty-three it was almost wild up here. All boats, open fields, and fishing. I like fishing. It's an optimistic hobby. It was good for her as a child; she had a good childhood. She liked the house; we all did. It was what I worked thirty years to have, and I got it. Paid it off two years ago; it's all ours now. That was what I wanted: a piece of land, a paid-up house, my own place. We're boxed in now, and the water's no good, and the fish are gone, and maybe I should have been told a paid-up house really isn't much for a man to want, but you believe what they tell you when you're young. It was a goal, as good as any, I suppose, and I got it."

He looked at me. "I didn't expect her to want to stay, though. They find out about life and they have to run off and grab for it fast because they've found out. It was right. It was my house, my land, I worked for it. It wasn't what she worked for. She had to go and do her own work. You just hope she won't get in too bad trouble. She could drown in the front yard. I wanted her to go. If I had another life, maybe I'd try for something else myself. Something I could take with me; like climbing a mountain or building a bridge in the jungle. Risk more, maybe. Only I hope she's all right."

The woman made the sound again. Then she closed her dark eyes. She seemed to sleep. Devine took a breath, unclasped his hands. They were squeezed white.

"As far as I know, she's all right," I said. "She may have lied to the police. If she did, she might be in danger. Not from the police. Tell me about the other two men."

"One was a small man, thin. Kind of sandy hair. He came early before we were up. I didn't like him; he kept looking all around. I told him Carla wasn't here and hadn't been. He was a bit arrogant, but nervous. He didn't seem to know what to do after I told him she wasn't here. He finally asked if I knew where she was. I told him no, and shut the door on him."

"Did he have a car?"

"A green sedan, old. He seemed uneasy when he left."

I described Walter Radford. "Was he like that?"

"Well, I'm not sure. I would have said older, but I'm not certain."

"The second man?" I said.

Devine shook his head slowly. "Very different. That was when we began to worry. Two of them, and then what this second man was like. He looked like some animal, a bear. He hardly spoke at all. Just said her name: Carla."

"Short, broad, with big hands and shoulders like a bull?"

"That's him. I told him Carla wasn't here. He pushed me away like a feather and went through the whole house. After he looked, he left. I thought of the police, but what had he done?"

"Did you tell either of them where they could find her?"

"No. I don't know anywhere except her apartment with the girls."

"Do you know a boy with a gray coupe? Thin, pale, long hair?"

"No."

Mrs. Devine opened her eyes. "There was a boy like that. He came here with her once. He called a few times after."

She got up and went out of the room. Devine and I sat. There were noises out of sight: drawers being opened and closed; the sound of rummaging. Then she came back. She carried a torn scrap of paper. She gave it to me.

"It was in a drawer with her things," she said.

She sat down again in the same chair and closed her eyes. Devine watched her. I looked at the scrap of paper. It had a name and address: Ben Marno, 2 Grove Mews, 5-B.

I stood up, and Devine watched me.

"She'll be all right," I said. "If she comes home, or calls, send her to the police. Make her go."

"Yeh," Devine said. "I will."

I went out to my car. As I drove away, the house was as clean and neat as when I had arrived. But it seemed smaller.

18

I RACED the black clouds down from City Island and lost. When I pulled onto the Triborough Bridge, the interlude of sun was over, and the river was gray below. Downstream the lights were on in all the tall buildings. The wind came up, and a driving snow had started when I stopped around the corner from the East Sixty-third Street building.

I was crossing the lobby when Walter Radford and Deirdre Fallon came out of the elevator. She had changed to a black sheath, but her sable was the same. I wondered if Carla Devine had a sable. What was better, a quiet Cape Cod cottage or a sable? If I knew the answer to that, I'd be rich—or in an insane asylum. Walter wore a dinner jacket and a cashmere overcoat and looked like an adolescent going to a formal.

"Is there any way to keep you away from us?" Walter said.

"No."

Walter reddened and clenched those anemic fists again. It seemed to be his reflex to any insult of any degree. Someday it would get him hurt. Deirdre Fallon touched his arm. He jerked back like a puppet. Maybe that's what he was.

"Did you go looking for Carla Devine?" I asked.

"Go to hell," Walter said.

"I wasn't first at her parent's house. I wasn't even second. One of those ahead of me sounded like you."

"It wasn't. I didn't leave the apartment all day."

Deirdre Fallon said, "There were two others, Mr. Fortune?"

"Only one that I'm not sure of," I said.

I didn't need any unexplained characters, but that's the name of the game. You can work six months on a case, only to have it solved when some total stranger walks into a police station in Medicine Bow and confesses to ease his conscience.

"Then you know one of them?" Deirdre Fallon asked.

"An ape name Leo Zar. Baron's faithful retainer."

She shivered. "I've met him. He scares me."

We had walked while we talked and were outside by now. The snow came down horizontally on the wind. A black Jaguar drove up. A garage attendant jumped out and brought the keys to Walter. While Walter was tipping him, a silver Bentley glided to the curb behind the Jaguar. Carmine Costa got out. He walked toward us as smoothly as the Bentley drove.

"Miss Fallon, Mr. Radford," Costa said, and touched his hat. He grinned at me. "Hello, baby, any luck with the sleuthing?"

"All bad," I said.

Costa was immaculately dressed without a hint of either dressing up or dressing down. He looked more the aristocrat than Walter Radford did—to anyone who didn't know real aristocrats. The blond Strega materialized behind Costa. I hadn't seen the bodyguard-and-friend move from the car or anywhere else. The perfect shadow, unmoving behind his boss like a statue in the snow.

Costa sympathized with me. "I heard about Baron. Looks like you got sold a bill, baby. That Weiss will go away forever." He shuddered, and it wasn't the cold. It was the thought of prison. I watched him shake off the specter with an effort, and turn to Walter Radford. "How about a lift? I got some business to talk about."

"We have our own car, Mr. Costa," Deirdre Fallon said.

I said, "What business, Costa?"

"Not your business, baby."

"It is if it involves blackmail."

I'm told that for a peaceful man I take big chances. Maybe I do. Like most men with few muscles, I consider myself fast with the brains, and you have to feel courageous in some area. I'm a pretty brave man with words. Or maybe just a stupid man.

Costa's smile went away faster than it had come. I got a flash of the violence in him. Not the violence of the hood, but of the old master sergeant. He was breathing down at me before I saw him move. He stood nose to nose. I expected to hear him say, "You, soldier!" next. Quickly as he moved, Strega was quicker. I felt the silent blond muscleman at my left and almost behind me. Something touched my shoulder. It felt like a vise, but it was only fingers. Strega's fingers. They chewed at my shoulder like a lion's jaws.

"Strega!" Costa said. The fingers went away, but Strega's breath was still on my neck. Costa's was on my face. His voice strained through teeth that almost ground in rage.

"Never! You got me? Never say that. Not you, not anybody! I'll tear a man apart with my bare hands, but never call me no blackmailer!"

I got it. Extortion is the blood of the Mafia. Every man has his estimate of himself. For Costa the black beast in his brain was the Mafia of his countrymen, and the Mafia was what he would deny to the grave. It reminded me of a time when I sat in a bar in Little Italy and listened to a minor hood deny for three hours that Lucky Luciano had ever been in white slavery. Everything else, okay—drugs, extortion, murder—but not white slavery.

"I got you," I said. I was gritting my own teeth, and not from the garlic on Costa's breath. Strega's fingers had gone, but my shoulder wouldn't be alive again for an hour.

"Okay," Costa breathed, and breathed hard. "Okay."

I saw Deirdre Fallon watching Costa. Her face was blank, but there was a flare to her nostrils. She was breathing fast, too, and her eyes were those foggy tunnels. I didn't blame her. Costa looked pretty good mad. She shifted her eyes, and for a moment I thought she was looking at me. But she was looking past me. I guess I didn't look a match for Costa. I'm not.

"Okay," Costa said, breathed easier, got his smile back. But it still wasn't quite okay in his mind. He wasn't sure I believed him. So in a way I won. Brains over brawn. He had to explain. "If you got to know, baby, I got a land deal in mind. A man gets closed once, that's chance. He gets closed twice, that's stupid. They don't close down a solid citizen."

He stopped. The driving snow had begun to make us all look like snowmen. I knew why I stood there, and why Costa and Strega did, but I wondered why Deirdre Fallon and Walter Radford were still there. Maybe they just had to watch Costa work. I watched him realize that he was telling me what was none of my business. He shifted smoothly, turned to Walter.

"You've got a lot of land up in North Chester now. I'll buy a piece, build a solid club, you name the price. Or maybe we could go partners. Who closes Walter Radford up there?"

Walter opened his mouth and closed it slowly. I saw his hand twitch. Deirdre Fallon considered Costa, and a shrewd gleam came into her eyes. Walter's eyes just began to shine.

"Partners?" Walter said.

"All legal, and no risk. I'm the gambler. You make an investment. Officially you're clean, but the important people know."

Walter licked his lip. "Well, I . . ."

Deirdre Fallon said, "Why not come to the house, Mr. Costa? Walter's office. That's where he does business."

Costa touched his hat. "Monday?"

"Monday," Walter said. "At my office."

"We'll be there," Costa said. "About two-thirty?"

Deirdre Fallon glanced at the silent Strega. "Two-thirty will be fine, Mr. Costa. We'll expect both of you." She touched Walter Radford's arm. "We'll be late, Walter."

He nodded, and they started off. Deirdre Fallon looked back at me. "I hope you find Carla Devine, Mr. Fortune, and before Leo Zar does."

"I'll try," I said.

We watched them get into the Jaguar. Three snowmen. No one spoke, and no one was watching Walter Radford. Costa breathed:

"That's some woman, babies."

"You said it yourself, Costa," I said. "To her we're a lower breed of animal."

"I know, baby; only there's something about that one. I can smell it. The Radford stud don't measure up. Right, Strega?"

The blond man watched the Jaguar skid away. "He's not much."

"He's nothing," Costa said, and to me, "A lift somewhere, baby?"

"Downtown?" I said.

"Why not?"

Strega said, "We'll be late, Sarge."

"We got time," Costa said.

They walked me to the Bentley. The silver-gray car said a lot about Carmine Costa. In his own way he was a maverick—the ex-soldier and man first, the gambler and petty hood second. It made him dangerous because unpredictable. My neck crawled a little as I got into the back seat with him. Strega took the wheel. The car purred away from the curb. Strega drove carefully, almost cautiously. The bodyguard didn't have to prove anything.

Costa eyed me. "What's on your mind, baby?"

"How come you just happened by the apartment tonight?"

Costa smiled. "I ever need a shamus, I'll call you. Okay, we come in every Friday. I got old buddies, a club like. Traffic is light because of the snow starting, and Strega makes good time. We're early, so why not talk business? I got the idea today, and when I get an idea, I move. Time's all we got in this world."

It could be true, or it could be a fast story to cover what he would have talked about if I hadn't been there.

"You said you didn't know Paul Baron?"

"Only his name and rep."

"You're covered for Wednesday night, of course."

"At my place past five A.M. Solid citizens saw me."

"That's not much alibi, with back doors and all."

"Do I need an alibi, baby?"

"That depends on what else is dug up on Baron's killing."

Costa smiled. "You let me know when I need more."

"I will," I said. "How well did you know Carla Devine?"

"Never heard of her. But I heard of Leo Zar."

Strega spoke from the front seat, "Leo's bad, real bad."

It was the first time I had heard the silent blond man speak without being asked. Costa agreed with his bodyguard:

"You know anything Leo wants to know, baby, you be real careful. I wouldn't tangle with Leo myself. I'd shoot him in the belly before he got five feet from me."

"I'll be careful," I said. We were passing the main library with its silent lions on guard. Even they looked cold in the driving snow. "I get out here."

"Okay, baby, let me know how you make out."

I stood in the snow and watched the Bentley drive off. The people pushed all around me. They were aliens in a different world from Costa, Strega, the Radfords and Leo Zar.

I walked to the subway and rode back up to get my car.

19

THE WIND had died, the snow was falling straight and thick now, and the Fifth Street Club had just opened. It was as deserted as a losing team's locker room. The same bartender was shining glasses. He ignored me.

"I want to see Misty again," I said.

He polished. "Christ, you got nerve. Get lost."

"She was mad?"

"You should of said you was a snooper."

"Does Misty live in that apartment upstairs?"

The bartender polished glasses.

"Did she make all her shows late Wednesday?"

The bartender sighed. "Cops. What's with them? They think all barkeeps got nothin' to do 'ceptin snoop around?"

He had a point. "The real police asked the same questions?"

"What else? I told them, 'n' I'm telling you: I don't know nothing about Misty. And she ain't in yet tonight."

"Which cops talked to you?"

He arranged glasses. "You won't believe this, but some bartenders are hired to tend bar. I live in Bay Ridge. I got a wife and four kids. I don't know every cop in New York."

I left him talking to himself. It had to be Gazzo who was still asking questions. The Captain was a good cop.

I drove into the twisting streets of the old Village. Grove Street was dark and quiet with falling snow. Grove Mews was an alley through an archway. There was a six-story side wall of a building on one side, and a bank of buildings with recessed doors on the other. Number 2 was the second recessed doorway. I used my lighter in the dark entrance. Ben Marno's name was scrawled on the broken mailbox for 5-B.

I went up the narrow stairs and found 5-B at the end of a dirty stone hallway at the top. There was no sound inside. I knocked. No one came. No one came from anywhere. It was so quiet in the corridor I could hear my heart. I tried the door; it was locked. The window at the end of the corridor was almost beside me. I looked out.

The fire escape reached to a window inside 5-B. I climbed out into the snow and got my knees wet. The window of 5-B was closed but not locked. The apartment inside was dark. I pushed the window up and dropped inside.

I stood in a room with four studio beds covered with wild-colored throws and piled with psychedelic cushions. There were painted orange crates for chairs and tables. A spider web made of thick rope hung from the ceiling, with a giant yellow fake spider in it. The sweet, heavy odor of marijuana hung in the air—not recent, just there.

There were two other rooms.

The second was like the main room with the addition of a bookcase and an expensive Scott stereo system. I had seen that before— Village pads where $27.50 had gone into all the furniture, but $1500 had been spent for music, photographic equipment, books or painting supplies. Maybe that was the right way.

The third room was wall-to-wall mattresses. A room for wanderers to spend the nights out of the wind.

There was no one around, and no bodies.

I let myself out the front door and went back down to my car. It was still too early for Misty Dawn to be onstage. I stopped for a couple of hamburgers, and drove to my office. The snow was beginning to pile up again. Another ten hours of it, and the city would be in for a bad few days.

My office was warmer than usual. Snow had piled on the window ledge and partly sealed the gaps. I sat down and looked at the telephone. I wanted to call Marty, but that was still no good for either of us. I wanted to call Captain Gazzo, but if Gazzo had anything to tell, he would call me. So I called Agnes Moore. After all, she had paid me to work. I got no answer. The day was running down like a tired hour glass.

I was on my third cigarette, waiting until I was sure Misty Dawn would be at the club, when I heard the woman in the corridor outside. The hurrying click of a woman's heels.

My fellow tenants on the floor were two old gentlemen who sold special books; an agency for cooks and waiters; and an astrologist. The woman could be going to any of them, but at this hour I doubted it. I was right again.

Morgana Radford opened my door and stopped. I think her trouble was that she had never seen an office without a reception room. It was a shock to her to walk in on me. She wore a heavy brown cape that made her look like Florence Nightingale.

"Come in, Miss Radford," I said.

She recovered. She was used to working with the poor. When she sat down facing me, her face was as precise as it had been in her cell in North Chester, but her eyes were animated.

"Deirdre Fallon murdered my uncle, and Mother and Walter know it," she announced. She said it with finality, as if she had told me before and I had doubted it.

"What makes you think so?"

"Ever since you came up, I've been watching and listening. My own investigation, you might say."

"That was you on the extension up there when I called?"

"Yes, but listen to me. I've watched them talking a lot, Mother and Walter. Always in secret when they didn't know I could see them. Yesterday afternoon I saw them arguing violently just before Deirdre left the house to come to New York. Walter went and got his Jaguar and followed her. He's watching her!"

"Yesterday? Thursday?"

"Yes, a few hours after the funeral. She drove off in that red Fiat, and Walter followed her. I think he lost her, because he came back in less than an hour."

I thought about Walter Radford's mood today. "What makes you think that means Miss Fallon killed your uncle? Why do they have to be arguing about her at all?"

"What else would they argue about now? Mother is probably defending Deirdre! Do you know about her?"

"Do I know what?"

Her righteous eyes gleamed nastily. "Mother told me all about it today. To keep me from learning about Deirdre in the wrong way, Mother said. I knew Deirdre was corrupt!"

She was a woman with a mission, and she used words like "corrupt" and "evil" too much. There is a sickness about people who love those words. Somewhere inside they love corruption and evil, love to think about corruption and evil.

"If you mean her past," I said, "I know about it. So does Walter. She doesn't seem to be hiding it."

"She's clever. She took them all in with her supposed candor. They think it makes her honest, but I see the darkness in her. I can see her holding herself in. There's something in her that she can't control, something animal."

"You think that whatever that is, it led her to kill your uncle? Why? He liked her, you said so yourself."

She brushed at the air, brushing away logic and answers. "I don't know, perhaps he learned something about her. I know that Mother and Walter are worried, tense. I think Deirdre has some hold on Mother."

She was a busybody, a meddler with a hobbyhorse. She was protecting her Walter, and she had more of her ruthless ancestors in her than she knew. It had simply been channeled in her into redemption instead of exploitation. That was not new, and a fanatic redeemer could be as deadly as any exploiter.

"What hold, Miss Radford?" I said. "If she killed Jonathan, I'd figure the hold to be the other way around."

"Then why is Mother worried? Why would she protect Deirdre?"

The words hung there in the office, accusing her. She had trapped herself. She had started by insisting that Gertrude Radford's actions proved that Deirdre Fallon had killed Jonathan, and now she was saying that Mrs. Radford's actions were all wrong if Deirdre had killed Jonathan. She had accused her mother of defending a murderer, now she asked why her mother would defend a murderer.

"Yeh," I said, "why? I don't think she'd protect Miss Fallon if she thought Miss Fallon had killed anyone."

I expected her to fold, but she didn't. There was a great deal of the Radford steel in her. She sat and looked at me.

"Very well, perhaps Mother doesn't know about Deirdre, but she knows something," she said grimly. "Mother came to New York on Monday night, quite late and alone. Mother never goes into the city alone at night."

"Monday? After the murder was discovered?"

"Yes. That night, of all nights, she would never have left the house without some urgent reason. She was waiting to hear again from Walter and George with the police."

"How'd you find out? You didn't mention it before."

"I didn't know until today. I told you I was watching Mother. I knew she had gone out that night, but I had assumed it was to visit some local friend. She hadn't even dressed, just put her coat on over her housedress. But today I remembered that she had had a phone call just before she went out. I questioned MacLeod, the butler. He likes me; we think a lot alike. He said he had driven Mother to the eight-twenty train that night. He said she came home late by taxi."

"Have you asked her about it?"

"No. She never mentioned going anywhere. She would only lie."

"What kind of coat was she wearing?"

"Her mink. A red housedress."

"All right," I said, "anything else you've dug up?"

She shook her head. She stood up. But she didn't move to go. "They'll destroy him, Mr. Fortune. Deirdre will destroy Walter. I know it. I know that, somehow, she killed Jonathan, and she'll destroy Walter."

"She couldn't have killed your uncle," I said. "She had no reason, and she has an alibi. It's impossible."

"I don't care about that. Somehow, she did it. I don't know how. I don't care about the facts. The facts are wrong."

"Maybe they are," I said. "Do you know a Carmine Costa? Misty Dawn? Maybe Paul Baron?"

"No."

"All right. Keep in touch, okay?"

She nodded. "Yes. Yes, of course."

I watched her go out, and let out a slow breath. Somewhere inside Morgana Radford was on the edge. Maybe it was only that she knew she would lose her last hope of having her Walter back once he married Deirdre Fallon. She was right about that. Deirdre Fallon would make Walter dance her tune, and Walter would love every minute of it. I didn't think she was right about much else.

No, her conclusions from her watching didn't hold water, but that did not mean that her observations were necessarily wrong. She had seen what she had seen, and I wanted to know where Gertrude Radford had gone on Monday night.

Then I heard the footsteps in the corridor. They were not Morgana Radford coming back. They were one man moving softly. I made it to the door on my toes and turned the lock. I listened. He was still at the far end of the corridor. (There is one big advantage to a creaky old building like mine—it creaks.) He could be stalking someone else, some other office, but "could" is not something to stake your health on.

I went to my file for my ancient cannon. It wasn't there. I had left it in my apartment. I headed for the window. People who want to talk don't creep up. At least, that's a good rule to go by. I went out the window. If I was wrong, all I would do is look foolish later. Looking foolish is never fatal.

On the window ledge I did not look down. I knew what was down there—a narrow black shaft with no visible bottom. I knew what was above, too. When your work is digging into other men's affairs, it pays to know how to get out by the window. Another advantage of an ancient building is that all kinds of braces, gingerbread, and ledges stick out of the outside walls.

I gripped an iron brace and hauled up to the middle window frame; caught hold of a deep crevice and hoisted to the slab ledge at the top of the window. From there I hooked my chin over another protruding iron brace and groped for the edge of the roof above. I got a good grip on a piece of gingerbread decoration, and pulled myself up until I could kneel on the iron brace. I wrapped my arm over the roof parapet, hauled, and flopped over the parapet into the snow of the roof.

Below, my office door crashed in. He would spot the open window. I ran for the next roof. I skipped the first three ways down from the roofs because the exits from those buildings were near the door of my building, and my visitor might not have come alone. I made the fourth roof before I heard him behind me. I went down through the fourth building and did not stop until I reached the bottom. I listened. He was still behind me up above. I went out into Eighth Avenue.

I had planned to blend into the crowd. There was no crowd. The wind had risen, the snow had thinned out, and it blew down the avenue that stretched empty like a deserted tundra. I ran right, dove down some steps into a narrow passage beneath the buildings, and ran through and up to the backyards behind my building. I looked for a weapon. All I could find was a pile of loose bricks. I grabbed one, flattened against the dark wall to the right of where the steps came up from the passage, and waited.

A minute passed. Then three. Slower than the slowest rocket countdown. Five minutes. Nothing moved anywhere. He was not coming. Ten minutes. I dropped the brick, climbed some fences, and went out through another cellar passage into Twenty-seventh Street. I flagged a cruising taxi.

20

AFTER A TIME, the taxi driver looked back at me.

"Where to, buddy, or did you just come in to get warm?"

It was a good question. Where to? Misty Dawn? Carla Devine? It was well known by now that I was interested in both of those ladies.

"Grand Central," I said.

The driver made a vicious turn uptown, and I sat back to think. Leo Zar? That was guess number one. Leo was looking for Carla Devine, and so was I. I knew he was, so he probably knew I was. It was not a pleasant guess, but the others were worse. If it had not been Leo chasing me, then I had no real idea who it had been. Ignorance is the big danger. It could have been anyone: Costa; one of the Radfords or a hired hand; maybe that unknown third man asking around about Carla Devine; or even one of Carla's friends, maybe Ben Marno. It had to be about the Radford affair. I wasn't worth killing, or at least maiming, for any other reason. I had no illusions about what my pursuer had had in mind. He had come softly, kicked in my door, and chased in silence.

At Grand Central I paid the driver and went to work. I had no picture, but Gertrude Radford was easy to describe: if she had taken a taxi, and if anyone remembered. My main hope was the fact that taxi drivers are a breed who work on habit, and the same cabs work Grand Central day in and day out. It took me the better part of two hours to talk to a lot of drivers with bad memories. I jumped at shadows the whole time. There is no future to working scared. In my work you have to assume that you are smarter than the enemy, and two jumps ahead at all times, or take up selling shoes. Careful but not nervous. It's easy to say.

By the end of the second hour I had my nerves more or less under control, and I got lucky. The twenty-second driver I braced leaned back in his cab and said:

"I remember. You a cop?

"Private. You're sure you remember?"

"I said so, mister. Let's see the license."

I've said it before—don't sneer at luck. Chance, fortune, accident, it does exist. While it's true, in a sense, that men make their own luck, by things like having the gall to question twenty-two cab drivers about something that happened for a few minutes five days ago, there is still, and forever, an area of pure chance. Sometimes I think that's all there is.

The driver gave me my license back. "She was dressed funny. In some long red thing with a mink over it. She didn't have no bag. She paid me out of her pocket with a twenty. Grand Central's an interesting stand, I watch, you know? She was my only real nut of the night. If she'd been a chick, I'd of figured she ran out on some guy, or got tossed out. But she was an old bag. White hair and no hat. Skinny. Nerved up. I was thinking about the cops. I mean, maybe she'd run out of some nuthouse."

"Where'd you take her?"

"East Sixteenth Street. You want me to take you?"

"Take me."

The driver made good time. I suppose I was his nut for that night. He probably had a lot of fun imagining the crazy lives of his passengers. As far as I could tell, no one followed us, and we soon pulled up in front of a tall apartment house near Third Avenue. I gave the driver an extra five. He drove off without looking back. Later, he'd build it all up for friends.

I found the name I expected on the bank of mailboxes in the lobby: Baron Paul Ragotzy. The name was engraved in script on an elegant calling card in the European style. This, then, had been Paul Baron's main residence. The space was a penthouse. That could mean more good luck for me. Staff members notice the action around penthouses, and this building was an older one with an operator-controlled elevator. (Self-service elevators have played hell with a good source of information.)

This operator was a young fellow with clear, alert eyes and an intelligent face. He saw I had more on my mind than a quick trip upward. His slender brown hands held the door open.

"Can I help you, sir?"

"If you can give me some information."

"If I have it, and it's ethical," he said. He hooked back the doors and sat down on his stool. I stepped into the car. He let the doors remain open. He had nothing to hide.

"Were you on duty last Monday night about nine-thirty?"

"Yes."

"There was a woman, about sixty but white-haired. She was wearing a mink and a red housedress and no hat."

"I remember her," he said, "a lady. She had good manners. We don't get many like her. You want to know where she went?"

"That's the question."

"Police?"

He eyed my missing arm. I showed him my credentials. He read them carefully, with interest. He gave them back.

"The police were here. They didn't ask about Monday. They asked about Tuesday and Wednesday."

"About Paul Baron? I mean, Baron Ragotzy."

"Yes."

"Then this woman went to the Baron's penthouse?"

"Yes."

"Alone?"

"Yes."

"Did she come here often?"

"I never saw her before."

"How long did she stay?"

"About an hour."

"Did she come down alone, too?"

"Yes."

"Did you see her with the Baron?"

"No."

I thought it over. At about 8:00 P.M. on Monday, Gertrude Radford had gotten a telephone call. She had come to see Paul Baron. That was hours after she knew that Jonathan had been murdered, and at a time when no one in the Radford family was supposed to have known that Paul Baron was involved except Walter Radford and Deirdre Fallon. And she denied knowing Paul Baron.

"How long had the Baron lived here?"

"A year or so. He was away a lot."

"He lived here alone?"

"Yes. He had a lot of guests. They sometimes stayed a time."

"Women?"

"Those who stayed were usually women."

"Anyone special? Regular?"

"Quite a few were regular. I couldn't say how special they were."

I described every woman I could think of in the case: Misty Dawn, Carla Devine, Deirdre Fallon, Morgana Radford and Agnes Moore—clients have lied to me before.

"All of them could have been among the women," he said. "I remember a couple of redheads as being pretty regular, and that small, dark, young one you mentioned was regular. She was sort of new, the dark kid. I can't do any better, it's a big building. The elevators keep pretty busy."

"How about men?" I asked. I described Costa and Strega, and saw no recognition. I pictured Walter Radford and George Ames for him, and then tried the unknown sandy-haired man looking for Carla Devine, and the thin, pale boy in the gray coupe. For good measure I threw in MacLeod the butler.

He shook his head. "He didn't usually have men up alone. They came in groups. Poker games, I think." He smiled again. "I guess I don't notice the men as much."

"I know what you mean," I said. "When did the Baron come in that night? I mean on Monday."

"I don't come on until nine. I never saw him."

"Then you don't know who else was up there?"

"I didn't see anyone."

"Who was on earlier?"

"The afternoon men. I doubt if they'd know much, though. They're both old guys, and they don't pay much attention to the tenants. Between five and eight is our busiest time, both cars run then."

"I'll try them tomorrow anyway," I said, and I reached into my pocket.

"I get paid," he said.

I thanked him and went out into Sixteenth Street. The snow had stopped completely again, and the temperature was going down fast. I walked down to Stuyvesant Park at the end of the block. I sat on a bench in the cold and lighted a cigarette. The park was deserted except for a lone man walking his dog. The man had a bushy mustache, and the dog, a golden retriever, pulled him along. The man looked frozen, but the dog was eager. A good man, who walked his dog no matter how cold it was.

I had my first clear lie. Gertrude Radford had gone to see Baron on Monday night, suddenly and in a hurry. Why? My theory said that Baron might have tried to go on with the blackmail after killing Jonathan. But Monday was too soon. He would have been lying low while he worked at framing Weiss. So Mrs. Radford had gone to Baron for another reason, or Baron had not killed Jonathan. The telephone call that had sent her to Baron made it sound as if Baron had not been afraid to contact Gertrude Radford.

Then why had he worked to frame Weiss? For someone else: the missing partner who had sent Weiss the message to contact me? Baron covered for his partner, but the partner couldn't take the risk so killed Baron who knew too much? Except I did not see a man like Baron trusting a killer, even a partner, so much that he sent away Leo Zar at a vital moment. Baron would not have been easily tricked by someone he knew had killed, and he had been tricked badly.

When two don't work, try three. A third person killed Jonathan. Baron knew it. The trusted partner killed Baron. Why and who? I had a feeling that they went together, the why and the who. If I knew who I'd know why, and if I could find out why I'd know who.

If Baron hadn't killed Jonathan after all, someone else had despite the facts and alibis, as Morgana Radford had said. The facts were wrong, and Baron had been covering for someone else. Then Baron had been tricked. That was the key: Baron's murder.

I stamped out my cigarette and went up to Third Avenue to find a taxi.

21

THE TAXI DROPPED me in Sheridan Square. I walked with the Friday-night crowd. They were all bundled up and eager, the girls like bright teddy bears in the cold and the neon lights. Here and there a determined maverick walked bold in a thin jacket and scarf, defying the elements and the world.

I left the Square and walked down the dark side streets. I was alone in a different world. The windows of the buildings were lighted, but they were a universe away to me where I walked. Grove Street was empty, and Grove Mews was a dark tunnel. Through its archway the Mews looked like a deserted medieval courtyard.

The snow lay white and thick and almost untouched in the Mews. I climbed the stairs to the stone corridor of the fifth floor of building number Two. An icy blast of wind greeted me. I had not closed the corridor window the first time, and no one had closed it since.

A sound came to me on the wind.

A light, flat, slapping sound in a slow, steady rhythm. Flat yet resonant. The funereal beat of a distant drum. Soft, like the muffled drums behind the gun carriage at a hero's lament. But not a normal drum: the tone was too flat, the beat too light. A weak and infinitely solitary sound on the wind.

I stepped to the door of 5-B. The door was half open, and the slow drumming came from inside. I pushed the door all the way open. The thin, pale boy whom I had last seen driving the gray coupe with Carla Devine in it sat on one of the studio couches. He didn't seem to notice me. There was no one else in the room. I closed the door behind me.

Ben Marno, if that was who the boy was, sat with his back against the wall, his legs straight out in front of him, and the small drum between his thighs. He wore dirty chino pants much too thin for a New York winter, and an old army field jacket as thin as the pants. His shoulders were hunched as if he had been cold all his life. His wild hair hung down over his face so that all I could see was his nose, his taut mouth, and his sharp chin. He was softly beating out the slow rhythm of the drum as if he hardly knew that his hands were moving.

The explanation of the strangeness of the light, flat sound of the drum became clear to me. It was an Israeli drum, or an Arab drum— they are much the same, Israeli and Arab drums, which proves that custom and culture rise from time and place and are harder to control than politics. It was about the size of a small bongo, made of earthenware like a jar, one end covered with a laced skin, the other end smaller and open.

"Marno?" I said.

He looked up at me, without surprise or curiosity. He looked, but I was not sure he could see or cared if he saw me or not. Indifferent eyes, and his hands never stopped their slow beating of the drum.

"Where's Carla?" I said.

His inanimate eyes, lumps of dark brown dirt, turned up to the grotesque false spider web on the ceiling, infinitely bored. Not with me alone, with it all. Flat, dead, unconcerned. Yet his hands went on and on in their soft, mourning rhythm, and there was something else in the dead eyes—shock, maybe? His hands here and alive, but all the rest of him withdrawn, gone somewhere else deep inside him.

"Where is she, Marno?"

His eyes stared at me. Then flickered, faintly, somewhere to his left. A small movement of the dark eyes. Toward the door to the next room. A reflex, involuntary, as if my voice had finally penetrated deep into wherever he was, and something had stirred momentarily.

I went into the next room. She was there.

She lay grotesquely with one thin arm and one perfect slim leg off a studio couch. She wore only a thin blue nylon robe, her child's hard and perfect little body still beautiful in death. Her eyes were open and wide without pupils, and a thin trickle of blood from her mouth had dried on her chin. She had bitten her tongue at the instant of death, as if death had come in some great shock wave. It had. There was no pain on her madonna face, only the contortion of some powerful blow from inside her frail body. I had seen the results of a massive overdose of heroin before.

I checked her arm, but I did not have to see the tiny, bruised puncture at the vein to know. There were other puncture marks, not too many. She had not been on the junk long or too steadily. Just long enough. It could be an accident, junkies died every day from overdoses. Or it could be suicide. But I knew it was neither of these; it was murder. Only there was no way I would ever prove that.

I lifted her from the grotesque position, laid her on the couch, and covered her with the blue robe. I went back out to Ben Marno. He sat where I had left him, staring at nothing, beating out the funeral dirge on his slow drum.

"How long?" I said.

His fingers stroked the drum. He looked at me. He was back in the present, in the spider-web room, perhaps because now I also knew what only he had known a few minutes earlier.

"Who knows?" he said. His voice was hoarse and thin. "Who cares? How long, he says. Forever, mister."

"I was here about four hours ago."

"I wasn't. I come back maybe an hour ago. She was here. Like you see."

"And you just left her there?"

"Stupid. Stupid kid."

"Like that you left her lying? A piece of meat?"

His fingers never stopped tapping their dirge. He bent his head, listened to the intricate beat, concentrated on his work.

"Lay her out, dad? Fold her hands, close her eyes, dress her in her best rags? Propaganda. She's dead, dad, the propaganda don't make no never mind to her no more."

His fingers did a slow, difficult run on the drum. He nodded to himself, pleased. "Who knows, maybe she can hear? Valhalla. You think there's a Valhalla for little tramps? Everything she wanted, and no payoff time?"

"All right," I said. "Mourn your own way, but . . ."

He silenced the drum with the flat of his hand. "Sympathy, dad? Lay it on me. I got a bad break. She was a nice little bird. Now I got to find me a new one. How's that for a rotten break for old Ben Marno?"

He had been hurt a lot more than anyone would ever know. He had been cut open, and he was bleeding alone. And he was not bleeding for himself, but for the dead girl-child in the next room.

"Who supports me now? Man, that bird did me one big bad turn. How about that? Who buys the groceries for Ben Marno?"

He was bleeding in buckets. Maybe if he kept it up long enough, he might even begin to forget in a week or so.

I said, "Who killed her, Marno?"

"Killed? A mistake. Too much H for one small bird."

"Killed," I said, "and no mistake. Who?"

His fingers began the erratic lament again. "Who, who! The big owl. Yeh. We all die, dads; we all get killed. It's a big burlesque, dads. Swatting flies."

"You said it," I said. "She was swatted like a fly."

"We're all flies, dads; we all get swatted sooner or later. So fly high, fly high!"

His voice and the beat of the drum rose, and I saw his eyes clearly for the first time. The pupils were small and tight, and the hysteria in him was not all grief. He was high on drugs, and there was something even more than drugs.

"You're high, Marno. Is that the way you get out of it?"

He did another quick run on the drum. "Just a little high, dads; not flying. Not enough. I didn't have enough, no. Ben Marno didn't have enough. Down to the last drop. So now I used it, the last drop, and no little bird to get more."

He was telling me something. I heard it. "She was out trying to get more for you? She took a big chance for you?"

"For me, for Ben Marno who had to have some more happy dust. So out she went to find a contact. She made it, dads." He threw the drum away. He looked at me from those constricted eyes. "Who, dads? You tell me. You're the detective."

"If you know that, you know more," I said.

"I know, dads, and I know nothing, right? She knew, and she knew nothing. Just enough to kill her. Very careful these men of action. My nice little friendly bird, but Paul Baron's chick because Paul Baron had what it took. So she was there, see? She didn't know anything, not really, but she knew that Baron was alive and kicking after this Weiss character walked out."

"She told you Paul Baron was okay after Weiss left Wednesday night?"

His eyes were dead. "She was scared, mister. Oh, God, was she one scared little bird. But for me she went out for a score, and I let her go! She'd been warned: clam up, keep out of sight. But she had a feeling the warning wasn't the end of it." He looked straight at me. "Not with you around. It was you, dads. She was sure the fuzz believed her, but she was scared that with you nosing around they wouldn't trust her. You and me, dads!"

What could I say? It was almost certainly the truth. So I said, "Tell me what she told you, Marno. All of it!"

On the studio couch he blinked at me. He drew his knees up to his chin, clasped his ankles. "What's to tell? She didn't know anything, but they killed her anyway! All she knew was that Baron had a squeeze on a kid named Walter Radford. She was part of the squeeze, a witness. Baron lowered the boom on the kid on Sunday. Only on Monday it all changed. Baron was all excited, and told her to cover for him for an hour. The deal was bigger, he didn't need her in it anymore. Wednesday they had dinner. Baron was happy as a kid, it was going like silk. Later she met him at his Fifth Street pad. Weiss showed up and got paid for some stupid bet and left. Baron was laughing, she says, after Weiss walked out. He sent her home right after. She figured he was expecting someone. She saw a guy watching downstairs, but she didn't think anything of it then. Next day this woman told her to clam up—tight. Not a word to the cops. She didn't know why. She didn't know that until the fuzz rousted her Thursday night when you were there."

"Woman?" I said. "What woman warned her?"

"She never told me."

"Think!"

He shook his head. "No luck, dads; she didn't want me to know. Too dangerous for little Ben to know. I figure it had to be someone tight with Paul Baron. Maybe it was that Misty Dawn. She was Baron's steady before Carla. It was the Dawn chick who started the whole play, Carla said. Seems Misty was close to some guy who knew Walter Radford, and she told Baron about the setup."

The room was so quiet I could hear voices far off on Seventh Avenue. Someone laughed somewhere out in the snow.

"Baron made his move on Sunday?" I said. "You're sure?"

"That's what Carla said."

I started for the door. "When you call the police, don't mention me."

"Police? Hell, dad, I'm fading away. Erase the name on the mailbox and fly. We're all islands."

He'd bleed a long time. Maybe even longer than Gerald Devine and his silent wife up there in their paid-off house.

I went down to the snow-covered courtyard and through the archway to Grove Street. I turned left for Seventh Avenue to find a telephone booth. I saw the car across the street and behind me as I turned toward the avenue.

A green car, its engine muffled by the snow, that eased away from the curb and started after me.

22

I WALKED a little faster.

The green car moved a little faster.

In the center of the block a tall apartment building stood dark with a shadowed alley beside it. The street was deserted. Beyond the tall building there was light at the corner of Bedford, and a block farther the traffic and people of Seventh Avenue.

The car squealed tires in snow and came up on me. As I began to run, I was sure I saw a figure in a doorway across the street. I had no time to take a second look. The green car was almost up to me, timing its move to the exact moment when I would be in the shadow of the single tall building.

I dropped flat in the snow.

Something seemed to spit in the silent air. A sharp, brief, almost contemptuous spitting sound. Brick chips cracked out of the wall of the tall building. Something whined echoing down the alley.

The car was past me. It braked, skidded in the snow, stopped and was already turning.

I was up.

The street was too narrow for a U-turn. The car climbed the sidewalk. It spat at me again. A window broke somewhere—as if distant, tinkling in the cold night air. The car engine raced, its wheels spinning in snow as it reversed.

I ran.

Back the way I had come, with no time to look again, or think, to see if there had been someone in that doorway across the street.

I ran and felt unreal, my feet silent in the new snow like the feet of a ghost. Only my breathing was real—loud breathing like a panting rabbit with the dogs closing in.

I passed the archway into the Mews and reached the next corner. The car roared up behind, no longer careful. I made the corner, went around, skidded, and sprawled flat on my back. My legs kicked for a hold to get up.

The car failed to make the turn any better, slewed sideways, and slammed up over the far curb and into an iron railing. I slid and scrambled up. The car raced its engine. Its bumper was locked into the railing. Its wheels screamed in the night, digging deep into the snow, turning uselessly.

I banged my face into a wall, bounced off, ran, and ahead saw the lights of a restaurant and bar. The Golden Donkey. I knew the Golden Donkey. I reached the door. Two men came out of the stalled car across the street. One fell into the snow, staggered up, fell again. I got the door of the restaurant open.

I ran through the dining room. Faces turned, gaped. A waiter raised his hands. I was by him. Behind me dishes fell, smashed. I was in the kitchen, and out into the night of the back alley. There were doors. I tried them. One after the other; running from one to the other. They were all locked. I turned the corner of the L-shaped alley. Ahead the next street parallel to Grove Street was quiet in the lighted rectangle where the alley ended.

I came out of the alley.

were there.

Spread out in the street, black figures against the snow, they trotted toward the alley. They, too, had known the Golden Donkey. They came on, men with something in their right hands.

The taller was in the lead, running at me. A face I could not see. Teeth that caught the stray light of a street lamp. A heavy, dark overcoat, its skirts flapping. A hat. A gun held forward.

I turned for the alley.

Shots hammered the night. Suddenly and heavy, like a blow against my ears in the narrow street and thin, cold air. Two shots. There was a scream. High and terrible like the scream of a wounded mountain lion. I went down in the snow, rolled, but it was not me who had screamed.

I rolled, unhit, and came half up, crouched in the snow with my lips back and my teeth bared in an animal snarl. As I came back up, I thought I heard another heavy shot, and two short, slapping sounds. The silenced gun that had shot at me. I was never sure.

Then it was over.

People were gathering from the dark air. There was a police whistle somewhere close. The smaller of the two who had been hunting me lay in the street. Another man lay beyond him against a building. Far off, a block away, a man was running hard. As I stood, he vanished.

I stumbled to the first body. He lay on his back. The front of his overcoat was torn out over bloody holes I could have put both fists in. He was a small, thin man. His hat lay in the snow. He had sandy hair. He was dead.

I pushed past people who gave me room. I had never seen the thin, sandy-haired man before, but I knew he had been the man who had gone before me to City Island to look for Carla Devine. I shouldered through the crowd around the second man who lay close to a dark building. I had seen him before. Leo Zar.

There were two small, neat holes close together in his chest. The overcoat was hardly torn. He breathed; slow and hard; uneven and rattling deep in his punctured chest. I bent down close to his broad, ugly face.

"Zar? Who were they? Zar!"

He breathed, rasping. His small eyes were shut. He was busy, concentrating, trying to live. His fists were clenched, the massive hands holding hard with all his strength to the air. A .45 automatic lay in the snow.

"Leo," I said. "Who were they? You were after them."

The cords in his bull neck, and in his wrists, stood out. His eyelids fluttered, but his eyes did not open.

". . . wife . . . Paul's . . . she . . ."

His barrel chest heaved, rested, then heaved once more in a deep, long breath. His eyes opened. He looked up into my face. His voice was deep and thick with the rasp of gravel.

"Get the damned bitch."

His breathing stopped. His cold eyes seemed to watch me, puzzled. He took one more ragged breath. His eyes glared up at me with pure hate. Hate that was not for me, but only for the life still in me. I was alive. Then he died, the last hate fading out of his bitter eyes.

Behind me someone giggled. Someone moaned, afraid. I stood up. A policeman was running up. I walked away and ducked into the alley behind the Golden Donkey. No one stopped me. I found a doorway and sat in its shelter inside the alley. I lighted a cigarette. I was not shaking; I was thinking, clearly, that I had finally heard Leo Zar speak.

I smoked. Paul Baron's wife. Leo had said that Baron had had a wife. He had said, it seemed, that the wife had somehow killed Baron. Yet Leo had been chasing two men. A dying man says what is important. Or does he? A dying man says only what his dying mind thinks. What is important, and what is true, when a man is dying?

When my cigarette was smoked out, I stood up and went back to the rear door of the Golden Donkey. In the restaurant they were all excited. They stared at me. I was a sodden mess. No one spoke to me, and no one stopped me going through.

I walked to Seventh Avenue this time without trouble.

The show was on at the Fifth Street Club. I had two quick shots of Irish and watched it from the bar. My nerves were jumping now at the sound of a glass hitting the bar. Someone who had little left to lose didn't want me around. One more murder was not going to make a hell of a lot of difference. I drowned my nerves in the whisky, thought that at least the someone was running scared, and concentrated on the show.

The line was six girls wearing just about what girls wear on any beach these days, but there was a big difference in the effect to watch them prancing in a room filled with fully dressed people eating. They did a vigorous bump-and-grind routine, and then went into the lead-in for the star. Misty Dawn was the star.

She appeared at center stage with a flourish. She was worth looking at. She wore more than the girls of the line, but all that did was focus attention to the right places. She bounced where she should bounce, and was hard where she should be hard. Her belly looked like ribbed steel, and moved like a powerful spring. Her face was all pancake, rouge, eye shadow, false lashes, eye liner and lipstick. The face was a mask: a ritual mask passed down through generations of girl-shows.

She was not a bad dancer, and her voice was deep, loud, only a little hoarse when she sang, and as boldly suggestive as it was supposed to be. But, watching closely now, I saw something else. I heard a nuance. She was deftly burlesquing her own act. She was putting them on, the drooling audience. Just enough to amuse herself and those in the know, but not enough to offend the true droolers. She was acting, playing a part and a private game.

When she finished, she ran off in a neat parody of every stripper who ever pranced into the wings like a mare in heat. The stage lights dimmed, and the interim show came on: an overage boy who played gaudy piano and sang in a whisky baritone. I paid and went through the curtain at the side. At the end of a long corridor an old man sat on a chair guarding the portals. I told him I wanted to see Misty, and he shuffled off with the message. He came back at the same shuffle.

"She's gone out."

That ended it for him. He sat down again and picked up his copy of *Playboy*. Girls trotted around the passage with less on them than they wore onstage. The world of night clubs does not breed modesty. For all I embarrassed them, I might have been a water cooler. Maybe that is true modesty.

"Out where?" I said to the old man. "Doesn't she have a couple of more shows?"

"Next in half an hour," the old man said, uninterested.

I left him reading, or staring at the pictures of naked girls. The pictures seemed to excite him more than all the real flesh and blood around him. It's easier to dream from a distance, and paper girls don't laugh at an old man.

I went back through the club and out into the cold night. I watched even old ladies warily. With a show in half an hour, Misty would not have gone far. She could have eaten or had a drink in the club. I went into the vestibule of the apartment above the club. Everyone agreed that it was where Misty lived. I used the pressure-and-push trick on the downstairs door. When I had it open, I pressed the bell for the apartment where Paul Baron had died, and went fast to the basement door, down, and through to the steps up to the backyard.

The fire escape of the old building was above me. I climbed it to the landing outside the window of the apartment. She was there, seated in a flowered armchair facing the door, her back to me. The room was dim, but I could see her fine legs in the black mesh tights. I could also see the gun in her hand aimed at the closed outside door. It was a tiny, chromium-plated automatic.

The window was not locked, but I could never open it, climb in, and get to her in time. My nerves were still raw, and I didn't like it, but there are some chances I have to take once in a while. I got my fingers under the upper edge of the lower window frame and shoved as hard as I could.

The window flew up as I said, "Drop it, Misty! I'll shoot if you turn a hair!"

Reflex was the danger. Her shoulders hunched.

"Drop it!"

The moment passed. She dropped the tiny pistol. It bounced away from her feet. I scrambled in through the window. She turned. Even in the dim light she saw my lone hand as empty as the day I was born. She swooped at the pistol. I made a wild dive. It was almost a dead heat, but I hit her in the dive, knocked her away, and fell on the gun.

I came up with it in my hand. (For some reason women will rarely dive to get something. They will bend, stoop. Maybe it is only the deeply ingrained consciousness of skirts, and the reflex response of not wanting to end up with their bellies exposed.) She went back to the chair and sat down. A cool woman. I waved the gun.

"What were you going to do with this?" I asked.

"Wait for someone to come to the door. Tell him to get lost. If he broke in, kill him. It's my place, I've got a permit, and a woman has a right to protect herself."

I listened to her hoarse voice. It was good. And she was good. She was also right. If she shot a man as she had said, she wouldn't even have gone to trial.

"Did you kill Baron to take over the blackmail?" I said. "Or was there another reason?"

"You figure it all out."

"The first thing I'm trying to figure is why you hired me, Agnes," I said. "That's your real name, right? Agnes Moore?"

Her masklike face was immobile. Then she reached for a package of cigarettes on the table beside the chair.

"That's right," she said. "Agnes Moore is my right name."

23

SHE SMOKED. I sat down.

"You want to start telling me?" I said.

She reached up and pulled off her red wig. Even with the short, dark hair of Agnes Moore in front of me, I would not have recognized her behind the mask of make-up. The Agnes Moore I had met had a round, scrubbed, almost mannish face. The main change was her voice. It was still low and strong, but all the hard hoarseness was gone.

"You're a pretty fair detective," she said. "I figure I give a good Misty Dawn act. No one except Paul really knew Misty and Agnes were the same, and he didn't tell you."

"You keep them separate all the time?"

She shrugged. "I'm an actress, a good one, but I have to eat. Misty is for groceries. I don't broadcast it."

"You said Jonathan told you about the blackmail," I said, "but Jonathan didn't know about the blackmail until Sunday, and you hadn't seen him since before Sunday. Only Baron, or someone working with him, could have told you. Then, tonight, a man told me that Misty Dawn was close to a man who knew Walter Radford very well. I put it together."

She nodded. "I had to be sure you connected Paul and Jonathan. I wanted the killer nailed."

"Did you?" I said. I handled the tiny pistol lightly, making sure she was aware of it. "Weiss contacted me right after I saw you. Someone had sent Weiss a message to contact me. He thought the message was from Baron, but Baron was already dead. Whoever sent that message knew that Baron was dead. I think you knew that Baron was dead when you hired me. I think you hired me to try to make sure Weiss was framed for all of it."

"Why the hell would I do that?"

"Where were you on Monday, Agnes? Between noon and three P.M.?"

"Where . . . ?" The mask of her face told me nothing. Her long leg began to swing. "Right here, buster. Right here."

"Alone?"

"After Paul left, yes."

"So you have no alibi. You knew all about the blackmail. You were very close to Jonathan Radford. Maybe you saw an easy opening. When Baron sent Weiss to collect, you followed Sammy. You went in the back way, or maybe Jonathan let you in. When Weiss arrived, you saw them fight. Jonathan went down, and Weiss ran. You grabbed the money, but Jonathan saw you, so you stabbed him. You got out okay, but you were afraid the police would find you if they didn't have a suspect. Weiss was made to order."

"You must be crazy!"

"Am I? Baron covered for someone, and it had to be someone he had a reason to help. You could have convinced him to help you. You could have gotten near enough to kill him easy. He would have felt safe enough with you to send Leo Zar away. I guess you just didn't trust him, did you?"

"Swell," she said. She laughed. Her leg was still swinging. "I double-crossed Paul, killed Jonathan and took the money, and then he framed Weiss for me? You didn't know Paul, did you? I loved him, damn me, but he wouldn't have gotten out of bed to save me or anyone who double-crossed him. He had his damned little Carla anyway. He'd have tried to get the money and then turned me in instead of Weiss. Paul wouldn't have helped anyone unless there was something in it for him."

"All right," I said. "I'm a reasonable man. You didn't kill Jonathan; Baron did. You knew he did. He . . ."

"Paul didn't kill him!" she broke in. "Paul didn't kill anyone!"

I ignored her. "He had his frame on Weiss, but maybe he was afraid of you, too. You just told me the kind of man Baron was; I believe you. If you knew he'd killed Jonathan, you'd have been afraid of him. So you killed him. Maybe he tried to use his knife on you to silence you, and you killed in self-defense. I'd believe that. After you killed him, you saw that Weiss could be framed for that, too. Baron had already planted the $25,000 on Weiss with that bet. So you got to me, told me about the blackmail in case I didn't know, and sent me out knowing that as soon as I heard Weiss's story I'd go looking for Baron. Your only risk was that someone would find Baron too soon, but there wasn't much chance of that. This is your apartment."

"Did you dream all this," she said, "or do you have some proof?"

"It was all smooth," I said, "except for Leo Zar. You didn't fool Leo, so you hired a couple of men to take care of him. They didn't get to him soon enough. He told me who killed Baron. He said Baron's wife killed Baron." I watched her as her black-mesh leg stopped swinging. "You were Baron's wife, weren't you, Agnes?"

"No," she said, and she leaned toward me. "Damn you, no! Paul wasn't married. I tried, at the beginning, but he laughed at me."

"Tell it straight, Agnes. The police will find out now."

"Paul didn't have a wife! Don't you think I'd know?"

She was a smart woman, tough and intelligent. She would know that she could not hide a marriage from the police once they knew what names to look for. It might take time, but they had the tools to track down a marriage. I sensed that she was telling the truth.

"How long were you with Baron?" I asked.

"Almost two years, off and on. Paul was never a one-woman man."

"And he never mentioned a wife?"

"No. He had a partner before I met him. A regular girl he worked with, but I didn't know her." Her voice grew bitter. "I don't think I met her. He had so many women. Maybe I met her."

"Then what did Leo Zar mean?"

"How do I know? Ask Leo."

"He's dead," I said. "So is Carla Devine."

She didn't cry out or shiver. She just seemed to shrink. Her bold, hard body became smaller, curled inward.

"What's happening?" she said. "A lousy little blackmail, that was all it was."

"It got bigger," I said. "Maybe you better tell me your side."

Her cigarette still burned in the ashtray. She lighted another without noticing. A cold blast blew into the room through the window I had not closed. I got up and closed it. She did not move. When I sat down again, she began to talk:

"When I met Jonathan, I saw right away that I could get him. He wanted me, he was rich, he didn't care what I was. Paul thought it was a great idea. Paul was like that; he got a kick out of knowing that other men had to pay for a girl he got by snapping his fingers. So I took up with the old man. He was a pretty good old man, I'll give him that. He treated me well. If I hadn't been hung up on Paul, maybe I would have treated him better. I wish I had. None of this would have happened. Paul would be alive."

She said it like that, without seeing the contradiction. She wished she could have been really Jonathan's woman, instead of Paul Baron's woman, but not for Jonathan—for Baron! It was Baron she thought about, even now.

"What did happen?" I said.

"Jonathan talked about his nephew, who was always gambling and losing. Jonathan kept buying the kid off, he said. I told Paul it looked like a good chance, set Walter up for a squeeze on Jonathan. Paul thought it was a great idea. He played the kid into a corner, got him to work with those girls, and you know the rest."

"He worked it alone?"

"No, he got some help, but I don't know who. He never told me how he worked his schemes."

"Go on."

She lighted a third cigarette from the second. "Paul made his move on Sunday. He figured the payoff would be Monday. He was here with me. He was waiting for a phone call. It came about eleven-thirty, or a little later. I could tell it wasn't what he'd expected. He went kind of pale, and ran out of here."

"The call was at eleven-thirty? You're sure? Not later, maybe one-thirty?"

"Maybe eleven-forty-five, no later. I was watching television."

"All right," I said.

"About one o'clock he called and told me to tell anyone who asked that he was with me until at least one P.M." She blew a thin stream of smoke. "I didn't hear from him again until I was in the club. He came around just after six. He told me to find Sammy Weiss, and to tell Weiss that Paul knew he was in a bind, and that Paul would help him. Weiss was to keep moving, stay on the loose, and check with Paul or Leo by phone every hour or so. I found Weiss and told him. That was it."

"That's all?"

"Everything I know," she said. She ground out her barely smoked cigarette. "Something happened after he left me Monday. I don't know what, but it all changed. He changed. I'd never seen Paul so excited as he was when he came to the club at six."

"The deal was bigger?" I said. "Better?"

"He was like a kid after the first kiss. The deal of his life, he said. Big. An annuity, he said. No piker $25,000." She looked at me. "And he wasn't scared or nervous. He hadn't killed anyone, believe me. He was flying high."

"Two days later he was dead."

She hunched forward in the armchair. "I didn't see him again until I came up here after the last show Wednesday. He was on the floor in the bedroom. There was blood. I ran. I didn't know who'd killed him, or why. I was scared. I went up to that Seventy-sixth Street place and laid low. Then I called you."

There was a silence in the dim room. The wind was shaking the windows. Even with the windows closed, a chill draft scoured the room through the loose window frames of the old building.

"You could have told all this before."

"Tell the cops I was tied into blackmail? Tell them I lied to cover Paul? Tell them I found him dead and didn't report it? I'm not so smart, but I'm not crazy. I'm not getting tied in to any of this. I'll deny telling you anything. But I want Paul's killer to burn, and that's why I hired you."

"He never said why he was so excited Monday night?"

"No."

"Did you see a knife, a wavy-bladed knife? A Malay kris?"

"You mean that Paul had? No, nothing like that."

I stood. "I'll have to tell the police."

"You've got nothing to tell. I said nothing."

She reached for still another cigarette and looked at the clock across the room. Soon she had another show to do, and a lot of shows after that: prancing with a big smile on a hot stage for drooling fools.

I laid her pistol on a table and walked to the door.

"Fortune," she said. "Get who killed Paul."

I nodded without turning around. I went out. Paul Baron had been a thief, a cheat, a liar, and a man who had probably never loved anyone in his life, but she had loved him. It's a harsh and stupid world. We don't worry about those who love us and suffer for it, we worry about those we love and who make us suffer.

Down on Fifth Street the Friday night crowds pushed around me. I went into a bar and found the telephone booth. I called Captain Gazzo. He was not glad to hear from me. I told him I wanted to talk to Sammy Weiss. He didn't like it, but after a short argument he agreed to let me. He was on his way out on a call, but he would leave instructions.

24

A GUARD TOOK me to the detention cell, and stood off. The guard was annoyed. My visit was irregular.

I stood at the bars. Weiss was lying on the lower bunk: a small, shapeless shadow; almost nonexistent. The dim shadow of a man who had never really lived, and who would leave no trace behind. When he saw me, he sat up, and his dark-circled eyes came into the light.

"How is it, Sammy?" I said.

"Not so bad," he said. "Not so bad."

I watched him. His voice was quiet, and he was not sweating. They say that adversity can make a man stronger, but I've seen trouble strengthen few men and ruin most. Yet Weiss sat there in the cell he had feared all his life without a twitch or a shiver. His deep, Levantine eyes looked straight at me, and his pale moon face was dry.

"I want you to think hard, Sammy," I said. "You said that Paul Baron got in touch with you about noon on Monday. You're sure it was noon? Not earlier?"

"Maybe after. Like I said, I was at the steam room like always. I had to take the call wearin' a towel in the hall."

"He knew you go to the Turkish bath every day at noon?"

"Everyone knows. Sammy Weiss, steamin' off the fat every day. Sammy the Slob. You got one crummy room, no family, no friends 'ceptin' bums like yourself, and nothin' to do except wait for the night action if you got a buck, so you pick up the routine so you got somewhere to go. Every day, and the steam don't do nothing at all."

"What did Baron say?"

He didn't hear me, or he heard something else inside him first. He stared at a dark corner of the cell. "I bought myself a corset one time. A man's corset, you know? Up in that lousy room squeezin' myself into that corset to make me a sharp-looking character. The easy way, the big fake. All a guy got to do he wants to look sharp is take care of himself and stop feeding his fat face. You looks in a mirror all your life, and you never sees."

Who can say for sure what goes on inside the mind of a man, any man? Or what can happen inside a man? Sometime during the long day and night Weiss had stopped sweating his eternal fear.

"Tell me exactly what Baron said on the phone, Sammy."

"He said I should go collect $25,000 from this Jonathan Radford around one-fifteen, not before that. It was worth $1000 for me. So I went. I was to take the money to his Sixteenth Street pad. Only this Radford started a brawl, and I never got the money. That's the truth."

"I believe you, Sammy. How long were you with Radford?"

"Maybe five minutes, a little more."

Five minutes. The mistakes we can make by assuming what we don't know but that seems logical.

"How did you feel when you walked into that study, Sammy?"

"Sweatin'. You know me. I been sweatin' all my life."

"Radford was at a window?"

"Like a big shot. In a bathrobe, giving me his back, you know? It was cold in there, but I'm sweatin'!"

"Now tell me exactly what happened. Details."

He shook his head. "I don't know, it happened so fast, you know? He stands there makin' me cool my heels a long time. I talk, he don't answer. I got hot and laid the muscle words on him. So he turns and jumps at me. We brawl, he goes down. I don't hardly touch him, but he goes down, and I run."

"Okay, Sammy. Was there a rug on the floor? Think."

"I don't know, Dan. Maybe there was a rug, maybe not."

"Did you see Baron again that day?"

"I didn't see him no time that day."

"All right, Sammy," I said. "Just sit tight."

He nodded slowly. "You know, since they locked me in here I been thinking. I mean, I know I didn't kill no one. Maybe they don't believe me, and maybe they never find out. Maybe I'm going up for it. But I know I didn't do nothing. I mean, I don't want to go away for the long fall, but maybe I can take it if I got to. I mean, I know I'm clean."

"You'll get out of here, Sammy," I said.

"Sure, Dan," he said, and he grinned. "I'll be here when you come for me."

The guard walked behind me as if he thought I still might try to break the archcriminal out to destroy society. He locked the corridor bars after I went through. The sound of steel against steel, like the clang of doom, seemed to give him pleasure. Prison guards are like that. I could never decide if they became guards because they were like that, or if being guards made them like it.

On the street I caught a taxi and went up to my apartment. I put my old pistol into my duffle coat pocket. I went back down to the rental car and started uptown.

George Ames answered the door of the East Sixty-third Street apartment. His theatrical face looked tired.

"You again?" Ames said. "I've talked to the police. The District Attorney is completely convinced of Weiss's guilt."

"District Attorneys are paid to be convinced."

"Are you determined to destroy our family?"

"I hope not the whole family."

I saw something in his eyes. Call it knowledge. Ames knew something, but I could not be sure what that was.

"Come in, then," he said.

I went in. There had been more changes. In another six months there would be no trace at all of Jonathan Radford.

"You're alone?" I asked Ames.

"Yes."

"Where is everyone?"

"North Chester. They plan to announce the engagement this weekend. I . . . I decided not to go," Ames said. "Would you care for a drink? I intend to have one."

"Irish, if you have it."

"Scotch, I'm afraid."

"It'll do." I sat down and watched him make the drinks. He gave me mine and sat facing me.

"Proceed, my dear Holmes," he said, and smiled. It was a try; a small attempt to lift the weight that hung on the room. It failed even for him.

"How much do you know about Paul Baron now?" I asked.

"I know the money wasn't a gambling debt, that this Baron was blackmailing Walter, or, rather, Jonathan."

"Did it occur to you that sending Weiss here was all wrong? For a debt, maybe. But not for blackmail. Why involve an outsider in a blackmail scheme?"

"I don't know. For safety, perhaps?"

"No, in blackmail, safety and success lie in how few people know about it. It would have been stupid to send Weiss here just for the money, and unnecessary." I took a drink. "Why did Paul Baron send Weiss? It's such an obvious question no one thought of asking it. Baron sent Weiss because he did, period. A self-evident fact. Baron did it. Only it isn't self-evident when you look at it. Baron had no real reason to send anyone for the money."

"How can you be sure of that? As you say, Baron did it."

"Baron made his move on Sunday. On Monday he was waiting for a telephone call. A call, not a messenger. He got the call at about eleven-thirty. It wasn't what he had expected to hear. He went off at a run. Only after that did he contact Weiss."

Ames watched his drink. "Where are you leading?"

"Tell me about Monday again. The morning."

He swirled the ice in his glass. "I had breakfast with Jonathan. I went to my rooms. At about eleven-thirty, a few minutes after, Walter came back. He said that Jonathan had gone out with Deirdre, and suggested we share a taxi as far as Grand Central. He took the train for North Chester. I went to my club."

"Where are your rooms?"

"In the rear. Of course, I have the whole place now."

"Your rooms are so separate that you didn't see or hear Walter or Miss Fallon, and you didn't see Jonathan go out?"

"The apartment is solidly built."

"So it comes down to the fact that after breakfast you saw and heard nothing. You didn't see Jonathan again."

He looked at me. "I'm tempted to say 'so what?' You knew that. Why bring it up?"

"Because no one who really knew Jonathan saw him after breakfast, except Walter and Deirdre Fallon."

If I expected a reaction, I didn't get it. His theatrical face was immobile. His eyes seemed to retreat into a distance inside his head. He waited, sipped at his drink.

I drank. "Weiss didn't know Jonathan. He was nervous, it all happened fast. He saw a man of the right build, in a bathrobe, and with a beard. Later he saw photographs of a body on the floor, and a dead man on an autopsy table.

"The doorman saw a man with a beard in Jonathan's clothes with Miss Fallon. It was cold. Jonathan would have been wearing an overcoat, a hat, maybe a scarf, the works. I'd bet my life that Jonathan walked past the doorman without speaking. Miss Fallon probably greeted the doorman, and maybe spoke to Jonathan as they passed. Illusion.

"At the restaurant it's Miss Fallon who's well-known. She probably introduced Jonathan. It's odds-on that the people at the Charles XII had never seen Jonathan before. Was he ever in that restaurant, Ames?"

"Not that I know. I'd say not."

I waited. He said nothing more. He sat and looked at his now empty whisky glass as if he wondered where the whisky had gone; as if he wished that more would somehow appear without the effort of moving, of getting up and pouring more.

"Do I have to say it?" I said. "Jonathan was dead before you left this apartment that morning."

"And the medical report?"

"A hundred variables could throw the M.E. off by an hour either way with Jonathan not found for so long. Cold, for instance. Weiss said the study was cold."

Ames stood and went to the whisky. "All the windows were open. I closed them."

"It didn't really matter that much, not with the body undiscovered until six o'clock. It was sure to remain hidden at least that long. Only you and Jonathan had keys, and you're a man of routine."

"So I am. No, Jonathan couldn't be found until I came home."

"Extra insurance," I said. "What counted was that witnesses, including Weiss, would say that Jonathan was alive as late as one-fifteen or even one-thirty if anyone believed Weiss." I finished my drink, set the glass away from me. "Weiss served two purposes, and maybe the frame-up wasn't even the first idea. First there was Weiss as a witness to prove Jonathan was alive at one-fifteen. That way everyone in the family was ruled out. The frame was another, better idea."

Ames carried his drink to his chair, and lighted a cigarette. "You're saying Jonathan was killed at eleven-thirty or so. Walter and I left. Paul Baron was called, and came here unseen. He then contacted Weiss, and also supplied an impostor to act as Jonathan. The impostor went to lunch with Deirdre, showed himself to the doorman, and was here to meet Weiss?"

"The impostor wore a bathrobe because Jonathan's right clothes were bloody. Baron had the impostor pick a brawl with Weiss. Weiss ran, Baron replaced the body and went out the back way with his faker. He got rid of the faker one way or another."

"One way or another? Yes, I see."

"Baron had removed the bloody rug and cleaned the floor."

Ames stared at me. "It strikes me as an involved scheme."

"No," I said. "Under the circumstances it was simple, almost foolproof. Baron knew a hundred drifters he could get in minutes, and who'd do almost anything for a thousand dollars. He knew Jonathan. All he needed was a man the right age and size. A beard can be supplied in ten minutes in midtown Manhattan. Once you were gone, he had no one to worry about who really knew Jonathan."

"But on the spur of the moment?"

"That's what makes me so sure. No one could have planned it in advance that well. He'd wait a year for just the right circumstances. It had to be spur of the moment; it grew out of the circumstances. He had a murder to cover fast. He had a body with a beard but otherwise ordinary enough, an empty apartment, and $25,000 on hand. It was just about all he could have done to fit the needs, and he found an impostor as easily as he found Weiss to play the patsy."

"How did he know he could get Weiss so quickly?"

"He didn't. Any messenger would have done. Pure chance."

"Why would Paul Baron do all that? Take such a risk?"

"Money, the big chance. He had a petty blackmail going, but once he had a murderer who let him cover and frame Weiss, he had a lifetime deal in his pocket. And he had the knife to back his play. That missing knife never sounded right. Now I know why it was missing. It had the killer's prints on it, and Baron took it."

"You mentioned a telephone call that, presumably, told Baron of the murder. As far as I can see, everyone here was his enemy, his victim. Why call him for help, and then help him?"

"Someone here was in with him. His partner all the way."

"Partner? Then you rule out Walter?"

"No. He could have let himself be squeezed to bleed Jonathan."

He moved and set his glass down carefully on the table. I watched him. I had no way of knowing how he was taking it all.

"You're toying with me, Fortune. You've talked in generalities, no names. You've mentioned Walter and Deirdre, but we all know they were here, they admit it. If what you think is true, then they must be involved in it, but not necessarily as murderers, correct?" He waited, but I said nothing. He stood up abruptly and went to the liquor bar. He poured a straight shot and drank it. His back to me, he leaned with both hands on the bar. "The way you describe it, someone else could have been here with Walter and Deirdre. Anyone. Unseen and unknown."

"A third person would have to have gotten past the doorman earlier, but it could have happened, yes."

He faced me. "Then there's me. I was here. It would all shield me, too."

"You were here," I said.

He continued to stare at me. Then he turned again, poured another shot, and downed it. He was holding himself rigid now. "What do you want me to do, Fortune?"

"Take a drive with me," I said. "It isn't just Jonathan anymore, Ames. Not even Jonathan and Baron. Two more bodies are on the list. One of them doesn't matter much, but the other was a stupid, scared little girl who never really started living. Now she's dead because she was just a possible threat to someone, and that someone is still running loose."

His back was a ramrod. "North Chester?"

"Yes. I have a car."

He turned. "All right."

He got his coat and hat and we went down to my car. I told him to drive. Even a man with two arms is pretty helpless when driving. I didn't think he had killed anyone, but that was theory and guesswork. I could be all wrong.

25

WE WENT ACROSS to the West Side Highway, passed the George Washington Bridge that was an endless moving stream of lights, and drove on through Riverdale to the north. Outside the city the snow was an unbroken expanse of white that reflected the lights of the rows of suburban houses and the colored neon of the shops and taverns.

Ames drove fast, skillfully, and in silence. The rigidity had not left him. He was a man with a lot on his mind, the effete aristocrat just about gone. He was offstage now, as much as any actor can ever be. I couldn't tell what he had on his mind, and he wasn't going to tell me. He was waiting, maybe only to find out what I really knew or had guessed, before he did anything. I didn't know what he knew, or had guessed, or how he felt about it. I didn't know how he would act when the time came to stop me or help me. Maybe Ames didn't know either.

We entered Westchester, and the houses were fewer. Only the traffic never lessened. The lights came on at me in a mass. I felt as if I were plunging through a dark tunnel with a million eyes watching me, alone with nothing but enemies. I was sure, now, that I knew what had happened on Monday morning, but I could never prove it unless I made someone panic. Panic can be dangerous, two-edged, but I had no other weapon.

By now Gazzo would be looking for me. Witnesses would have described the one-armed man who had been with Leo Zar when he died. Leo, and the death of Carla Devine, would give Gazzo some doubts about Weiss. He would want to talk to me. I didn't have a lot of time. Weiss had less time if I didn't produce a killer, with evidence, soon.

The D.A. would not have doubts. To the D.A., or some tenth assistant D.A. for Weiss, Carla Devine would have died by accident or suicide from depression over Baron's death, and Leo Zar would be the victim of a gang rumble. Sure, both deaths might be a result of Baron's death, but that didn't change Weiss's obvious guilt. Not a bit. The tenth assistant D.A. would get a good night's sleep. Chief McGuire would think about it longer, he would even instruct his men to keep their eyes open, but he had a whole giant city to police. McGuire's detectives wouldn't try too hard. Weiss probably belonged in jail anyway, and even Gazzo had too much work to do.

We passed through North Chester just after midnight. Five minutes later Ames turned the car into the long drive up to the fine old house with its two cottages behind. There were lights in the downstairs windows. Ames parked at the front door.

The butler, MacLeod, let us in. Mrs. Radford was in the library. Ames walked behind me as if his legs were heavy and his feet were mired in mud, his flamboyance noticeably missing. Gertrude Radford was alone. She closed her book, put it carefully aside, and acknowledged us:

"You came, George. I'm pleased. Mr. Fortune. Sit down."

I sat. Ames went to stand in a corner near an obvious liquor cabinet. Mrs. Radford's pale eyes watched Ames. She wore a gray lounging robe, and her white hair was immaculate. Her rings were on her fingers. A coffee cup stood on a crystal coaster on the table beside her. The library was neat, solid, orderly, with everything in its proper place. The ashtrays looked as if they had not been moved, or used, for a century.

"Could Walter and Miss Fallon join us?" I asked.

Her frail hands made a gesture, but her youthful face was smooth, and her fragile body was relaxed. I could have been a cousin she saw every week. There was a crease between her eyes that might have been worry, but didn't have to be.

"Forgive me, Mr. Fortune," she said, smiled. "I'm sure you want to get to your mission, whatever it is, but we always talk over a cup of coffee in the family. I find it a civilized custom, and feel lost without it. You prefer percolator, don't you?"

"That's fine," I said.

She nodded. "Three percolator, please, MacLeod."

"Two, Gertrude," Ames said. He opened the liquor cabinet and found the whisky.

Mrs. Radford said, "I think coffee would be better, George."

Ames poured a drink without answering her. She sighed, as if she would never understand men who needed the crutch of liquor.

"Two cups then, MacLeod," she said.

She folded her thin hands in her lap and sat smiling at me politely. She ignored Ames now. He stood in the corner, drinking. It was clear we were not going to discuss anything until the coffee came. We would not have discussed an imminent invasion before the coffee came. She held to her routines, to all the external realities of her life, no matter what. Her rock in an unpredictable sea.

MacLeod returned, and I accepted my cup. The coffee was still good. She sipped twice, and then set her cup down.

"Now, you wanted to see Walter and Deirdre?" she said.

"All of you," I said.

Her voice was neither warm nor cold, ordinary. "Deirdre has been out for some hours. She went alone, I don't know where. Walter should be in the house. MacLeod, find Mr. Walter and bring him here, would you, please?"

MacLeod left. Mrs. Radford sipped some more of the coffee, and her pale eyes studied me over the cup.

"You want to talk about Jonathan's murder again, of course," she said. "Have you learned something important?"

The tone of her quiet voice was normal, conversational, politely interested. So normal it was abnormal. We were not about to discuss some charity bazaar.

"Two more people have been murdered, Mrs. Radford. One was just a girl, a child who'd done nothing to anyone."

"That's awful, Mr. Fortune. Did I know her?"

"She was one of the girls your son worked with."

"It's a violent world," she said. "I am sorry."

"Sammy Weiss was in jail, Mrs. Radford."

"As he should be."

"Weiss couldn't have killed the girl and the other man."

"Obviously, of course," she said, and smiled. It was a gentle, pleasant smile. "What has all this to do with any of us here?"

"They were killed because of Paul Baron. And Baron was killed, at least in part, because he knew who really murdered Jonathan."

"Are you here to accuse someone?"

Her frail face still smiled politely, and her voice was matter-of-fact. She really wanted to know if I was there to make an accusation.

"I think you know damn well why I'm here," I said. "Your trip to New York on Monday says you know."

"Oh, get to the point. You've come to say you've found out that my son killed his uncle? You've come to accuse Walter?"

"I figured you knew," I said. "Yes, Walter killed Jonathan."

Ames put his glass down with a bang that echoed in the small library. "Damn it, Fortune, how can you be sure of such a thing? Walter had no motive. You agreed anyone could have been there!"

"What happened after Monday tells me, Ames," I said.

"After Monday?" Ames looked at me, and then at Mrs. Radford. He picked up his glass, drank.

"Mrs. Radford made a deal, Ames," I said. "A payoff to protect the killer. She wouldn't have done that for anyone but Walter. Only Walter makes sense out of the rest of it."

Ames squeezed his glass, said, "Gertrude?"

"Be quiet, George, for goodness' sake," Mrs. Radford said, and said to me, "What do you intend doing, Mr. Fortune?"

"My God, Gertrude!" Ames's theatrical face was ten years older. "You really knew, and . . ." He drank. Whisky dribbled down his shirt front. "Do you know what they did? Walter and this Baron? Tell her, Fortune! The whole fantastic story!"

"Please, George," she said. "I'm not the least interested."

I watched her smooth and youthful face that had never asked herself a question she could not answer, and I believed her. She didn't know how Weiss had been framed, and she didn't care. How Weiss took the fall for Walter didn't concern her, only that he did take it. Weiss was nothing, a zero, a convenience to be used for Radford-Ames survival. She did not care how Jonathan had died, or even that he was dead once it had happened. Jonathan, dead, did not matter. The family went on: a unit, a whole more than any single member.

She folded her frail hands. "Walter had a tragic accident. He acted foolishly afterward, yes, but he was frightened, and he knew that the authorities would not consider it the simple mistake it was. They would have persecuted him. He made a stupid arrangement, it seems, but I managed to correct that. Now, is this what you came to tell me, Mr. Fortune?"

"Among other things," I said.

"Then you've told me. I see no reason to bother anyone else. Walter has been disturbed quite enough."

"Is that all you have to tell me, Mrs. Radford?"

"Certainly. My late husband showed me how business functions. If you have some proof against Walter, tell me and we can discuss money and terms. If you have no proof, you can leave before I call our Chief of Police and have you arrested. You have no legal right to be here, I've investigated that. Do you have proof?"

"Jonathan's death may have been an accident, I think it was," I said. "The other three murders weren't accidents."

"Do you have proof, Mr. Fortune?"

Her pale eyes studied me, and what could I say? I had no proof yet. Ames came to my rescue for the moment. He set his third empty glass down, rubbed his pink, barbered face:

"Walter couldn't have killed Baron, Fortune. That much I know."

Mrs. Radford said, "Please tell him nothing, George."

Ames ignored her. "Walter really was with me at the apartment on Wednesday night. He never left."

"Did he make any telephone calls?" I asked.

"No, none. I remember because Deirdre made quite a few, and Walter was disturbed by that. He became angry at her calls."

"George!" Mrs. Radford said. "You're a fool!"

I finished my coffee, sat back in the chair. "Walter didn't kill Baron or the other two, Mrs. Radford. You did."

"Oh, don't be ridiculous! If you try to prove that . . ."

"Not by pulling a trigger," I said, "by making the deal you made on Monday night. You killed them as sure as if you had gone out and done it yourself. Your deal made it all happen."

I heard Ames pouring another drink. I didn't look at him. I was looking at Mrs. Radford. She didn't even blink at me. She shook her head:

"When a man buys something, he is not concerned with what others do to deliver it to him," she said firmly. "My late husband taught me that, too. I entered into an arrangement, I kept my side of the contract. I am in no way responsible for how others arranged to deliver their side. That is not my affair."

Ames said, croaked, "What arrangement?"

I could tell by his voice that he had at least guessed. Before I could do anything else, the butler, MacLeod, appeared in the doorway. Walter was not with him, but Morgana Radford was. She looked like she had not changed her clothes since I had last seen her, but there was an odd gleam in her eyes.

"Where's Walter?" I said to MacLeod.

Mrs. Radford waved me away. "Call the police, MacLeod. I have asked Mr. Fortune to leave; he has refused. Tell the Chief that I believe Mr. Fortune is armed."

MacLeod looked at me, and left. I stood up. Mrs. Radford knew damn well I'd never use the pistol. Morgana Radford looked at her mother, but she spoke to me:

"Walter went out to find Deirdre. I told him."

"Told him what, dear?" Mrs. Radford said.

"Where did he go?" I said.

Morgana didn't seem to hear either of us. She told it her own way. "I know Walter's been watching her. When Deirdre went out tonight,

Walter wasn't here, so I followed her. To that gambling house! She's gone there alone before. I told Walter. An hour ago. He ran out. Now he'll see her for what she is!"

The righteous, fanatical girl trembled where she stood with the rest of us watching her. There was something pitiful about her. She was going to save her golden little boy, destroy the evil witch, open Walter's spellbound eyes.

"Don't be juvenile, Morgana!" Mrs. Radford said. "I'm sure Deirdre knows just what she is doing. Walter is being foolish again."

In a way Mrs. Radford was a lot like Sammy Weiss. For Weiss it would all work out fine as long as he did nothing; his luck would change. For Gertrude Radford all one had to do was pay for something, buy someone, and everything was accomplished as she wanted it.

I walked to the door.

"Mr. Fortune!" Mrs. Radford snapped. "You will not bother Walter or Deirdre."

I looked back. "I'm sorry, Mrs. Radford. You've done enough damage. I don't take your orders."

"George!" she said. "Morgana, get MacLeod."

She turned to each of them. Ames poured another drink and looked at the floor. Morgana just stared at her mother. Neither of them moved. After a moment, Ames turned his back to the old woman, and to me. There was no anger on Mrs. Radford's smooth face, only amazement.

"Stop him," she said. "What's wrong with you? George?"

I left her and them. MacLeod did not appear to stop me. I went out to my car. I didn't have any doubt about what gambling house Morgana Radford had meant.

26

THE PARKING LOT of the big brown house was full of cars and empty of people. I saw Deirdre Fallon's red Fiat. I didn't see Walter Radford's Jaguar. The lot was dark and swept by the wind. A mist of dry snow blew like drifting sand across the open lot from mounds at the edges.

When I parked and got out, the scouring wind made sounds that played tricks with my nerves. I was a long way from my own backyard. Costa's silver Bentley was parked in its private space around the corner from the front entrance. I went inside.

The rooms were all going full blast, the elegant marks losing their money as fast as in any garage-floor crap game, if with more comfort and gentility. I stayed far in the background, my duffle coat on my arm. I did not see Walter or Deirdre Fallon. I chewed my lip for a time, then headed for the telephone booth inside the front door. I put on my coat and slid into the booth.

Costa's office number would be private, but the club should have a listed number. It did. I dialed and watched through the glass as a houseman ambled to a wall telephone. I asked for Costa. I saw the houseman hesitate. I gave my name and said it was urgent. He told me to wait. I watched him press a button, and my line went on hold. He pressed another button, and almost stood at attention as he spoke into the phone. He nodded, and my line went off hold.

"Hello, baby, what's up?" Costa's easy voice said.

"I want to talk to you."

"You know where to find me."

"No, somewhere a little more public. I'm at the railroad station. Just drive up slow; I'll see you."

There was a silence. When his voice came back on the line, it could have sliced steel. "You putting me on, Fortune?"

"You better come," I said. "Come right now, and come alone."

I hung up. In the booth I sat down where I could see both the front door and the curtained entrance to Costa's office. He had to come, if only to call my bluff. He appeared in less than two minutes, wearing a sleek black Chesterfield and an angry scowl. His coat bulged. He stopped to talk to the houseman. He was alone. I didn't see Strega anywhere. I was a two-bit private eye, and a cripple, and I had counted on his pride. He strode out the front door. I slipped from the booth and followed him.

Outside, I saw him just turning the corner toward the Bentley. I slipped to the corner and peered around. The Bentley was only some twenty feet away. I waited until he had the door open and was sliding behind the wheel. Then I sprinted the twenty feet.

He was so busy he didn't see me until I was leaning in the window, my old pistol in my hand. His black eyes looked up at me, and then he grinned. He curled a lip at my gun.

"Where'd you pick up the musket, baby?"

"I keep it around for courage," I said. "Keep your hands on the wheel, and face front until I'm in the back."

I slid into the back seat. His sleek black hair shined in the faint light reflected from the snow. He was watching me in the rear-view mirror, all his teeth flashing in the smile.

"You need courage, baby?" he asked in his easy voice.

"Someone is acting like I do," I said.

"The Radford thing?"

"Yes. Where are they, Costa? Walter Radford and Miss Fallon?"

"Why would I know, baby?"

"I think you know."

Costa moved. I pushed the pistol at him, but not too close. He put both his hands out in front of him.

"I like to see who I talk to, Fortune," he said. "My hands are open. My coat's buttoned. You got me alone. I'm turning."

He turned until he could rest his hands on the back of the front seat. He leaned against the door, his dark eyes on me. I sat back far out of range. A Bentley is a big, roomy car.

"You think I killed old Jonathan after all, baby?" he said.

"No, Walter Radford killed his uncle."

"So what's the pitch?"

"Walter didn't kill Paul Baron or the other two."

"What other two?"

"Leo Zar, and a girl named Carla Devine."

Even in the reflected light I saw his black eyes take on a hard sheen like well-polished ebony. He whistled through his teeth. I waited. Outside in the wind-swept parking lot no one appeared and nothing moved.

Costa said, "You think you know something, baby?"

"I know that after Walter killed Jonathan, Paul Baron came to his 'rescue' and set up a frame on Sammy Weiss. That gave Baron a real hold on Walter, with the murder knife as security. Or Baron thought it did. Mrs. Radford outfoxed him. She made a deal with his partner. So Baron got shot, and the other two were killed because they knew too much about the frame-up."

"Baron had a partner? You mean all along?"

"It's all that makes sense. Only someone Baron really trusted could have both killed him and set the second frame-up on Weiss. Someone who knew everything Baron was doing."

"Who, baby?"

"Deirdre Fallon," I said. "It has to be. She probably conned Walter into getting Baron to cover Jonathan's murder in the first place. She was there; she got the idea."

"I knew there was something about that one. It figures, yeh. She's smooth; she's been around. She didn't figure with Walter."

"No, she didn't figure until the small blackmail turned into a big squeeze. Then Mrs. Radford bought off the big squeeze. The pay-off was Walter himself. He was rich now, and he wanted Deirdre. All Deirdre had to do was get Baron out of the picture."

"You think Walter knew?"

"No, but maybe he's guessed by now."

Costa rubbed his jaw. "Did she have to kill Baron? That's taking a hell of a risk even for all Walter would have."

"She had to," I said, "but she didn't kill him. Not alone. She set him up and got a sucker to do the dirty work for her."

"A sucker?" His black eyes were down to points.

"Someone who wanted her, Costa. Maybe a share in the loot, but mostly for her, I figure." My hand sweated on the pistol.

"You think I'm dumb enough to kill for a woman, baby?"

"I gave up trying to figure what men will do for a woman a long time ago. There was an arranged frame-up on hand, maybe it looked foolproof," I said. "Where is she, Costa? Where's Walter?"

"I ain't seen them, baby. They're not around here."

"Her car's here."

"Here?" he said. "That Fiat?"

"In your lot over there."

"Damn, baby, you're ahead of me. I didn't see her tonight."

"She'll cross you," I said. "She'll get someone to kill you, or do it herself. She's in too deep. Baron and Leo Zar were both armed. They'll never prove Carla on anyone. You can take a plea. Manslaughter, or even self-defense."

His voice was all the way down to bare bone. "You take big chances for a cripple, baby."

I leaned. "Earlier tonight you said you didn't know Carla Devine. But when we were all up on Sixty-third Street Deirdre made sure you knew that Leo Zar and I were looking for Carla. I wondered why she said that out loud at the time. A few hours later, Carla Devine was dead. Then I knew. Deirdre was tipping you that Carla had to be silenced before Leo or I got to her."

"If she was tipping someone, baby, it wasn't . . ." He stopped. The hard shine went out of his eyes. I saw something like a quick fear in his eyes. He said, "Jesus!"

I said, "Strega. Where is he?"

He shook his head. "Around. He's supposed to be around."

"Where was he Wednesday night?"

"His night off," Costa said. He said it as if it hurt his mouth. "I ain't seen him around so much tonight. Listen, Fortune, you've got it all wrong. Strega wouldn't . . ."

"Where would he be with her, Costa?"

He watched me. Then he said, "Let's go."

He went first out of the Bentley. I followed. He went around the house. He made no attempt to get his gun, call out, or try any other tricks. As we reached the open grounds behind the house, he began to walk faster. I saw another house some hundred yards away across the wooded backyard.

"Where we live," Costa said. "Both of us. I got the top."

It was a small, two-story house. The path that led to it through the woods was almost untouched. A snow-packed dirt road curved to it from the highway. Costa began to run as we came near the house. He was pulling at his pistol now.

"Something's wrong!" Costa said.

The front door of the house was open. There was faint light somewhere to the rear. Costa ran through the open door, and I was right behind him. Inside, stairs led up from a narrow hallway. Costa ran past the stairs to the rear where another door was open, and light showed in the room behind the door.

The room was a bedroom. The bed was a tangle of sheets and blankets. A bottle and two partly filled glasses stood on a bureau. Two chairs were knocked over. The window near the bed was broken, and glass lay all over the floor under it. A woman's black dress hung on a chair. A pair of woman's knee boots lay on the floor. The stink of gunpowder hung in the air.

Strega sat on the floor with his back against the bed. He wore only a black silk Japanese kimono. It was torn, bloody. Blood was pooled on the floor. There was a pistol in Strega's right hand. His eyes were open, his face was chalk-white, and his blond hair was dark and matted with sweat. Costa dropped to his knees in front of Strega. The handsome gambler kneeled in the pool of blood. He didn't notice.

"Strega! Kid! Baby!"

"He's dead, Costa," I said.

Costa didn't seem to hear me. He was massaging Strega's limp hand. I looked around. The story was easy to see. The low and muted light, the bottle and glasses, the rumpled bed, and Strega's kimono told it all. The window told the end of it. Someone had shot through the closed window. It was no more than ten feet from where Strega sat. One shot had smashed a mirror. Three had hit Strega.

Costa stood and went to the telephone. The knees of his trousers were sticky with blood. Costa picked up the receiver and stopped.

"He's dead, Costa," I said.

Costa didn't answer. He stood with the receiver in his hand. I went to the window. There was blood in the snow, and a trail of trampled snow led to the dirt road at the side of the house.

Costa said, "He never could handle women. Funny, a big guy like Strega. The women, they always ruined him."

I went and picked the pistol out of Strega's dead hand. It was a long-barreled .38. It had just been fired. It showed the marks where a silencer had been fitted.

"A sucker for women," Costa said. And he began to cry.

I began to search the room. I wrapped the .38 in one of Strega's T-shirts and put it into my coat pocket. I searched some more, and finally found the knife, the kris, hidden under some shirts. It was wrapped carefully in tissue. There was a .45 caliber automatic with it. The .45 had been fired recently. I wrapped the .45 in a T-shirt, too, and put it in my pocket. The pocket sagged. I put the kris in my inside jacket pocket.

Costa was kneeling in front of the dead man again. Big tears poured down his dark, handsome face. I left him, and the house, and walked through the woods to my car. I saw that the red Fiat was still parked in the lot.

As I drove from the lot, a police cruiser passed me on its way in. It had North Chester markings. They were not going to worry about technicalities like town lines when they had a favor to do for Mrs. Radford. They were after me, but they would find Strega and Costa sooner or later.

I drove as fast as a one-armed man can drive with control.

27

THERE WAS LIGHT downstairs in the Radford house, and the Jaguar was parked in front. I walked up the front steps with my pistol in my hand. The front door stood open. MacLeod was not in sight. The living room was deserted. I went along to the library.

George Ames sat in a leather wing-back chair. He held a glass, and an almost empty bottle stood on the table beside the chair. His quick eyes were numb with whisky, or numb with something else. He was not drunk.

"Have a drink," he said.

"Where are they?"

He drank, licked his lips. "I think I'll sell the apartment, go and live at the club. I never was much good at this kind of reality. I've been sitting trying to think of what I can do, but there isn't anything. I don't want to do anything." He drank again. "Our fault, I suppose. Jonathan and Gertrude mostly, but the whole family. Something missing in Walter. No control, no judgment, just his desires."

"I don't know," I said. "How much did you know?"

"Nothing, but I had wondered. Vaguely. About the marriage. The idea of marriage had never come up, as far as I knew. I'd not heard it mentioned. Walter wanted Deirdre, yes, but I hadn't thought that she wanted him. She seemed so uninvolved, toying with him. I would have said that marriage had never crossed her mind. She seemed too, well, mature for Walter. Too cool."

"Until Monday."

"Yes, Monday. You know, Jonathan did like her, but marriage is another matter. Deirdre is modern, free. She made no secret of her, shall we say, independence. I don't think Jonathan would have liked the marriage. I'm not sure Gertrude would have before it . . . happened."

"But it looked like a neat way out of trouble, and maybe Deirdre would have been a good wife for Walter," I said. "Where are they, Ames?"

"In her cottage. Have one drink. I'm waiting for a taxi. I really can't do anything here. I need my routine."

"No, thanks," I said.

I went out and along the hall to the front door. Outside, I looked into the Jaguar. The front seat next to the driver's seat was a mess of blood. I walked around the house. Morgana's cottage was dark. The other cottage showed low, muted light. I walked toward it through the snow. The wind had dropped, and a deep silence filled the cold vacuum of the night.

Music came to meet me from the cottage, the massive tones of a symphony. I knew it: Sibelius's Second Symphony. The last movement, the theme that always carries for me the vision of a solitary horseman riding from far off across a frozen wasteland. A man alone in the universe.

Inside, the cottage was identical to Morgana's cottage. The music came from a stereo in the far corner. One light burned in the elegant living room. Deirdre Fallon lay on a couch, her eyes closed, and her delicate face intent on the music. She wore the long sable coat, and no shoes or stockings.

She opened her eyes. "I had a feeling you would cause trouble. Paul should have killed you."

"I didn't do much."

"Just enough to unbalance it," she said. Her finishing-school voice was speculative. "It's odd, but I'd still like you to tell me about your arm. We never change, do we?"

"Where's Walter?"

She closed her eyes and lay back. "In the bedroom."

I walked into the bedroom. A lush bedroom not at all like Morgana's monkish cell. She was there, Morgana, slumped on the floor with her head on the bed. She was crying. Mrs. Radford was not crying. She sat erect in a chair, her smooth face calm under the perfect white hair.

Walter lay on the bed. He was dead. He looked like a boy, but he did not look golden. There was terror in his eyes, and pain. He had been shot in the stomach, and he lay curled up like a punished infant. There was a lot of blood, even with all he had left in the Jaguar.

"A job well done, Mr. Fortune?" Gertrude Radford said.

"No," I said. "I wanted him alive. He's no help dead."

Her pale eyes moved to look at Walter. "I couldn't protect him from his own stupidity. No mother can."

"Your deal killed him," I said.

She shook her head. "I'm not responsible for my son being a fool over a woman. I made a logical arrangement, and he ruined it. I'll make you an offer. I'll pay for your silence, and for any evidence you may have. I'd rather Walter's mistakes remained as unknown as possible."

"Don't waste money on me," I said. "With a little pressure, the police will keep it quiet for free. Everyone's dead."

I thought I saw a tear trickle down her face, but I wasn't sure. She'd have a lot to bury in routine and coffee. She'd bury it. She'd bind her wounds, and blame everyone but herself. I wasn't so sure about Morgana. The girl had not moved. She knew more about pain, and she had lost more. In her crusade to save Walter, she had been right. She had opened the eyes of her golden boy, and had killed him by it. Coffee would not help her.

I went back to the living room. Deirdre Fallon had not moved. The music was building to its conclusion. The solitary horseman rode toward his destiny.

"Answer some questions?" I said.

"Quiet, please," she said, her eyes closed.

I waited. I like Sibelius. It's hard music, austere, like a man alone on a giant rock asking questions of the sky. There are no answers, but the questions make us men.

The music faded away in a long, hovering note. She opened her eyes. "What questions?"

"You and Baron planned to blackmail Jonathan all along. Walter never knew. He thought you were his girl, not Baron's partner. Baron made his pitch on Sunday, and on Monday you and Walter went to Jonathan to get the money. He had it there. What happened? He changed his mind? He refused the money?"

It was hard to think of blackmail and murder when I listened to her soft voice, watched her beautiful face.

"He said Walter could rot in jail. He called Walter a corrupt infant. He pushed Walter, he slapped him. Walter picked up the knife. It was over in seconds. Poor Walter."

I waited, but she didn't go on. She wasn't going to give me much. Why should she? I said, "It was about eleven-thirty. You got Walter and Ames out. At first you probably just planned to cover Walter, give him an alibi. You called Baron. He came in the back. He had the idea of Weiss and an impostor to make it look like Jonathan was still alive long after Walter was on the train. Then one of you saw the bigger deal, probably you. You've got the brains."

She said nothing. I wasn't sure she heard me. "The two of you made a list of the serial numbers of the $25,000, and wrote Weiss's name on the pad. You took the knife, and you had Walter cold. That night you called Mrs. Radford to tell her. It was you she came in to meet at Baron's penthouse. She made her offer: drop the blackmail and marry Walter. He wanted you. Everybody wins if you can handle Baron."

On the couch she reached for a cigarette. She seemed to be seeing a vision.

"The brass ring," I said. "She handed it to you. You never thought you had a chance with the Radfords, and Walter didn't move you much, but there it was. I guess she knew you. Maybe you'd shown her something in the months with Walter: hunger for all the Radfords had. For all they are. You could be a Radford. Walter would have money, position, even power. She had to play it fair all the way, you had the knife, and Walter wanted you."

Maybe it's an inevitable story in a country that makes the many want what only the few can have. For most the big dream can never happen, but the trying for it is supposed to make the world move. Maybe it does, I don't know. If I knew I'd be writing important books no one would read. What I do know is that every now and then there are some who, like a cheap gambler, want it now and easy and without work, and that ends in violence.

"So Baron had to go," I said. "He was no match for you, and he trusted you. He sent Leo away because he was only meeting you, his partner, that night. He met Strega and his .45 instead. Carla Devine almost queered it, but Strega spotted her. You should have killed her then, not warned her. Maybe you liked her."

She had closed her eyes again. I suppose I was right, Carla had reminded her of herself, and she wanted to forget that part.

"When did you marry Paul Baron?" I said.

She opened her eyes and turned, but she said nothing.

"You had a husband," I said. "You couldn't buy him off, or divorce him, because you couldn't even tell him about the deal. He would have owned you for life. He could tell Walter you'd been his partner. He knew Walter had killed Jonathan. And he'd have bigamy on you. He'd never have let you alone. No one seemed to know you were married to him, or that he was married at all. Who would look for an old marriage? So, kill him. Strega was there to do it for you, and Weiss would take that fall, too."

She spoke up to the ceiling, "I was fifteen when I met Paul. What I told you earlier was mostly true. The well-bred girl with no present and no future. Paul showed me how to live high and easy. I liked it. We were a good team. I never had an arrest. Then I married him. It was wrong; we were too different once the bloom was off. So we went our private ways, but we still worked together sometimes. A divorce didn't seem important. Not until Monday, and then it was too late. Mrs. Radford handed me the big chance. I had to have it. No one knew about Paul."

"Leo Zar knew. Maybe Paul told him, or maybe he had found out."

"We all make mistakes."

"You didn't make many. Did you plan to kill Strega, too?"

She raised herself on her elbow, and both blue eyes were straight toward me. "I killed no one. Remember that. There's nothing you can do to me."

She didn't blink, or look grim, or do anything but let her words sink in. Then she lay back again. "Strega was in love with me. He had wanted me ever since Walter first took me to Costa's place. I don't think it would have lasted long, though. Once I was married, he wouldn't be hard to ease away from, and after all, he had killed Paul, hadn't he?"

"Strega was a rough man."

"Rough men can be handled," she said, "only . . ."

"Only?" I said.

She sat up, and I had a flash of long, pale leg. She looked toward the record player. "We don't make the same mistake twice, we make it a hundred times. Rough men, strong men, that's my weakness. I can handle them, but I can't stay away from them. Walter was a boy. Tonight I went to tell Strega we'd have to stay apart for a time, to start the brushoff. But he wanted me. So, first him, and *then* the brushoff. Once more, you see?"

She drew on her cigarette, but it had gone out. She dropped it into an ashtray. "Walter was at the window. He shot Strega. Then he stood out there in the snow crying. He stood, and Strega shot him. I brought him home. I had it, the big rainbow, but it all turned to brass."

She stood up and went to put a record on the player. It was Brahms, his Fourth Symphony. I could hear Morgana Radford crying in the bedroom. There was no sound from Mrs. Radford. She was probably planning the funeral.

"What happened to the man who posed as Jonathan for you?"

"He ran with his money. Does it matter?"

"Who was the sandy-haired man looking for Carla?"

"No one. A gun Strega hired."

"Where's Walter's gun?"

"In the Jaguar." She began to nod her beautiful head in time to the powerful music. "There's nothing you can do, you know. Not a thing."

I walked out. I went through the snow back to the Jaguar and got Walter Radford's gun. It was a simple hunter's sidearm. Then I got into my car and started back for New York. I would tell Gazzo the story. He could handle the local police.

28

IT WAS MORNING out in the city. In Captain Gazzo's shade-drawn office it was still night. The dim light etched sharp shadows across Gazzo's gray hair and tired eyes. I had told my story some two hours earlier, and Gazzo had set the full machinery of his department in motion, and now he sat behind his old desk and brooded in his perpetual midnight.

"We can't touch her," Gazzo said at last.

"No. They're all dead."

Deirdre Fallon would not even be charged. There was nothing to charge her with. Everyone who could have testified to what she had done was dead. Mrs. Radford could tell nothing without admitting that she had concealed murder, and she was not going to do that. Mrs. Radford would not help the police. She had no first-hand proof anyway, George Ames had no proof, and all my evidence was against the dead.

I had given Gazzo the Malay kris, with Walter Radford's fingerprints still on it, for Jonathan's murder, and Walter's pistol for Strega's killing. Ballistics would do the rest. They had Strega's .45 automatic to prove who had killed Paul Baron, and Strega's .38 pistol for Leo Zar and Walter Radford. Costa had been contacted and had confirmed where I had found the weapons. Gazzo had taken my word that Strega, or his sandy-haired hired hand, had killed Carla Devine. We would never know which one had actually done it, or exactly how. Police work is rarely neat.

"I'll send Walter Radford's gun, and Strega's .38, up to North Chester. They'll handle those killings," Gazzo said. The Captain sighed a long, weary sigh that had thirty hard years of frustrating police work behind it. "They'll talk politely to the Fallon woman, and to Mrs. Radford, and then they'll turn them loose with an apology and their sympathies. A tragic love triangle. They can't prove anything else. We can work out the whole affair in detail, but there's nothing a ten-cent judge would let the D.A. get to a jury. She walks out like a bird."

"The mother, too," I said. "Women live longer."

Gazzo didn't laugh. "I'll put the word in for you with the North Chester police. You might want to work up there again. You stayed away from them to keep down the publicity on the Radfords. They might even thank you."

"What about the other favor? Freedman."

His gray eyes moved to consider me without friendliness, but without rancor either. The stubble on his tender face stood out like dirt on the face of a gravedigger. He toyed with Strega's .38 on the desk before him.

"It's been done. I guess Weiss has that much coming. Let's get down there."

We went down to the room where they processed prisoners who were being released. Sammy Weiss was already there. He was gathering up a small pile of debris they had taken from his pockets when he had been jailed, and counting the few dollars of his own he had had. The $25,000 was stolen property. Weiss didn't even ask about that money.

"Hey, Danny," he said to me. He grinned all over his moon face. His eyes were not grinning, not yet. A life sentence was still too close behind him like a dark, perched vulture.

"Good deal, Sammy," I said.

Gazzo said, "Take a lesson, Weiss."

"I learned, Captain, yeh."

He put his possessions and few dollars into his pockets. He stood there. All the police in the room watched him. I smiled. The police didn't smile. They had seen it all before, and they had seen too many like Weiss go out one day and come back the next.

"Well," Weiss said. He looked around. "That it, Captain?"

"That's it," Gazzo said. "You get home on your own."

"Ride in free, eh, only no free ride back?" Weiss joked. Even he didn't laugh. "It's okay, sure. I'm out, right?"

Still he did not move. It was as if the open door was too much. He was afraid to take that first step toward the open door because maybe that door would close in his face just as he got there. Doors always closed for Sammy Weiss.

We were all looking at that door when Detective Bert Freedman walked in through it. Freedman did not notice Weiss. He walked up to Gazzo.

"You wanted to see me, Captain?"

"Weiss is being released," Gazzo said.

Freedman let his eyes turn until he saw Weiss. His thick body became rigid, and those always-ready fists began to clench. A deep red color spread up his neck to his cold face. He stood that way for almost a full thirty seconds. Then he laughed:

"Maybe next time, bug. I get you next time."

Inside I was close to praying. I had wanted Weiss to have this moment over Freedman. I had wanted Freedman to be humbled by one of his victims. I had wanted too much. Whatever Weiss had found inside him in prison, he was still Sammy Weiss. He tried to meet Freedman's eyes, and failed. His flabby face began to sweat.

I said, "Someday, Freedman, you'll make a mistake, and hound a man too far, and it'll be your last mistake."

"You think so, Fortune?" Freedman said. "I think you better stay out of my beat."

"That's enough, Freedman," Gazzo said.

"No!" Weiss said, cried, almost shouted.

His voice was too loud, like a great croak. "No! I didn't do nothin', and you pushed me around. You don't push no innocent guys around no more! I got rights. You go make sure I done somethin' first, you hear?"

It wasn't much defiance, but for Weiss it was heroic. Freedman's red face turned scarlet, and his fists clenched tighter, but he said nothing. Weiss stood his ground and tried to square his fat shoulders. He didn't quite make it, but he took that first big step toward the open door. He went out through the door almost walking tall.

I went after him. He didn't wait for me. When I reached the sidewalk, he was a half block away and already starting to run in the cold morning sun. I watched him vanish.

He had had his small moment. I did not fool myself that it would last. Soon he would be the same Sammy Weiss back at the old stand—rooting for a shaky dollar, running from his shadow, and out to prove every second that next time he would ride the pot all the way. He wouldn't. That much change happens to few men this side of death.

Deirdre Fallon would pay for nothing she had done, and she would not try the same tricks again. Her excursion into violence had risen from a precise combination of circumstances that would not repeat. She was a smart girl; young and beautiful. The men would still fall over themselves to let her use them. She would be fine.

Mrs. Gertrude Radford would go on exactly the same; unhappy, maybe, but comfortable.

George Ames would forget.

There was little justice in it, and less morality, but as I stood in the snow and morning sun of the city I began to feel good. An innocent man was free. Weiss wasn't much, but he had been innocent, and better to let a thousand guilty escape than have one innocent man suffer. At least, that's what we're supposed to believe.

Weiss was free, Agnes Moore owed me some money, and my woman, Marty, would be back from Philadelphia soon. I felt fine.

It's a world of percentage and partial victories, and on the whole I figured that right had limped home a shade ahead this time.

THE END

Read the first chapter
of the next exciting Dan Fortune mystery

Night of the Toads
by Dennis Lynds
#3 in the Edgar Award-winning Dan Fortune mystery series

I'd never have remembered the girl if Ricardo Vega had been another man. He wasn't. He was "Rey" Vega to anyone who claimed to know him well – El Rey, the King.

We don't admit it, but we consider a successful man a better man. A prince of success, an inevitable winner. Maybe it's only that we never lost our need for princes, and if we don't have an aristocracy, we make one. An aristocracy is comforting. It takes us off the hook – we never really had a chance to make it big. At the same time of course, since an aristocracy of success isn't really closed to us, we can all dream. A contradiction, sure, but logic has never bothered people's attitudes much.

The trouble is that the successful man himself has a way of coming to believe he is better. From there it's an almost automatic step to believing he was always better – born better, a different breed of man. A man who should have rights and privileges ordinary men don't have, a special man, superior, a king. That was Vega. I didn't know him well enough to call him Rey, and he made me remember the girl.

It was one of those wet springs in New York when the streets are under water, and no collar can keep the rain out. All through March, when Marty came home with her show from Philadelphia, and through most of April, she was in a bad mood. She's Martine Adair, my girl. She wasn't born with the name, or with anything else that she cares about now, except, maybe, the ability to work hard and long for what she wants. She's an actress, and she's good. But being good isn't always easy, not when you want to be good more than you want to be known.

Her bad mood that April wasn't all the weather. She had trouble in her show. It came to be my trouble on another rainy Thursday in my small and gray bedroom.

"Go and kill him, Dan!" she said. "Right now!"

"Knife, gun, or my bare hand?" I said.

She sat up in the bed. A small woman with long red hair, and big eyes, and the face of a young boy. It's the combination of the boy-face on the woman's body that kills the men, including me. That and her eagerness. She vibrates when she's sitting motionless. Her walk is a stride, and her anger is fury.

"He should be dead!" she said. "He's got to die!"

"He will, honey. We all do."

She lighted a cigarette, and looked down at me by the light of the flame. "I mean it."

She did mean it. I saw it in her eyes: a cold, gripping fury. She wanted Ricardo Vega dead, destroyed. And no, she didn't mean it; not the normal, civilized Marty.

"It's my role, I worked for it," she went on at last. "Kurt says I'm good. He's the director. He says don't worry. But at the bank, Vega is the whole show, and I know it. I fought him off in Philly, I don't want to fight anymore. I want him to stop. I don't want him in my bed."

"Can Vega get you fired?"

"Of course, if he made an issue. I don't think he will."

"But you're not sure, baby?"

"I'm sure, and I'm not sure."

"So maybe you'll say 'yes' in the end?"

"Does that make you sick?" Her eyes flashed down at me, because her anger had to go somewhere. Then she touched me, and turned her face away again. She went on, "The key word is maybe. That's how they work, the important lechers, the big-scorers who have to have what they're supposed to want – every girl they meet. He's attractive, they always are: handsome, strong, a public figure. He's exciting, and he's nice, you know? He won't get a girl fired, of course not, but . . . ? Why should a girl risk even that small maybe when it really might be pleasant? Bingo! It's easy when a man knows how, has the weapons." Her voice was bitter in the gray evening light.

She has fine breasts. I watched her breasts, and the long hair thick on her shoulders. "What do you want, Marty?" I said.

"Tell him that he doesn't get me fired, and he doesn't get me. Hit him. Knock him down."

"With a club?"

"Scare him! You're a detective, Dan. Make him stop before I say 'Why not,' because I'm scared of losing it all."

"All right, Marty," I said.

She dropped her cigarette into the ashtray, lay close against me again. She was warm. "I worked so damned hard for this chance."

I knew how hard she'd worked for it, her first real role in a play, and after she had dressed and gone to her chorus rehearsal, I watched the rain for a while. When your woman asks you to act for her, you'd better act. At least, you'd better if you wanted her friendly for the next month. I didn't want to meet Ricardo Vega on those terms. I didn't want to go to Vega so she'd be nice to me later.

Yet I did want to meet Vega. I don't like men who trade on fear or hope; who scare or entice with their power to make or break dreams. So after a while I got up, dressed, and made myself think about that better reason for what I was going to do. By the time I had my raincoat on I'd worked up a good anger. No one should ever have to live scared.

Before I left to get a taxi, I picked up a book I'd been reading. Vega was a producer, director, investor of his own money as well as an actor, and a book in my hand might help me get past the door easier.

The taxi dropped me at Lexington and Eighty-first Street. As I walked, the rain seemed to come down harder. An elegant marquee sheltered the glass-and-chrome doors of Vega's building, and a uniformed doorman stood inside the doors. I walked on. My book wouldn't help me get inside if I had to let the doorman announce me.

I found the basement service entrance. It bristled with signs that warned undesirables. Opening the door, I padded quietly across the basement in case a super was around, and went up into the lobby. I was lucky, the door opened into a wing of the lobby out of the doorman's sight. The elevators were self-service. I took one up.

When I rang at Vega's door, I heard loud voices inside. I had to ring again. The door finally opened. Holding it was a rawboned blond man with a lean, rough face and hungry eyes. His boyish but battered face gave the impression of a traveled twenty-year-old, but he was older; maybe twenty-eight. He looked uncertainly at my wet raincoat, black beret, book, and empty left sleeve as if he didn't know what he was supposed to do next.

I helped him out. "I want to see Vega."

He shrugged. "I'm waitin' myself."

"Fine," I said, and pushed past him. "That makes two of us."

Meet the Author: Dennis Lynds

A raconteur and Renaissance man, Dennis Lynds changed the mystery form and along the way created colorful private detectives who consistently won awards as well as the hearts of readers. He was a tall, lanky man with a nose the size of Gibraltar and a generous nature that made him a soft touch for friends, panhandlers, and his children. He published some 40 novels under various pseudonyms, won awards such as the Edgar, the mystery world's highest honor, and received accolades from legendary authors like Ross Macdonald. "A novelist of power and quality, ... one of the major imaginative creators in the crime field," Macdonald wrote of him.

The New York Times named several of Lynds's novels to its Best Mysteries of the Year lists. Remarkably, two of them written under different pseudonyms appeared on the same list – *Silent Scream* by Michael Collins and *Circle of Fire* by Mark Sadler.

Amused, Lynds said that none of the *Times* editors realized he was both Collins and Sadler. "I don't think they ever figured it out," he explained. And he never bothered to tell them.

Seldom does an author change the course of a genre once; rarely twice. Lynds is credited with being the writer who, in the late 1960s and early 1970s, propelled the detective novel into the Modern Age. His most famous pen name was Michael Collins. With that name, he created the opinionated Dan Fortune, the star of one of America's longest-running private detective series. The first book, *Act of Fear*, won the Edgar Allan Poe Award for Best First Novel. "Many critics believe Dan Fortune to be the culmination of a maturing process that transformed the private eye from the naturalistic Spade (Dashiell Hammett) through the romantic Marlowe (Raymond Chandler) and the psychological Archer (Ross Macdonald) to the sociological Fortune," according to *Private Eyes: 101 Knights* by Robert Baker and Michael Nietzel.

At heart, Lynds was a rebel. Two decades later, he rattled mystery critics and changed the field again, this time by introducing literary techniques into the genre, beginning in the late 1980s with *Red Rosa, Castrato*, and *Chasing Eights*, and continuing well into the 1990s with *The Irishman's Horse, Cassandra in Red*, and *The Cadillac Cowboy*. Other authors followed, proving the flexibility and durability of the suspense world. "No one could accuse *Lynds+ of reworking the same turf in his novels. ... His last several books have pushed the private-eye form into some fascinating new shapes," according to *The Wall Street Journal* in 2000. *The Los Angeles Times* commented, "It takes style to bring that off. Bravery, too, of course."

Lynds also published mainstream novels, short stories, and poetry. Five of his literary short stories were honored in *Best American Short Stories*.

During World War II, he was a rifleman and carried books of poetry in his knapsack as he fought across France. He was a strong swimmer, so when he and fellow infantrymen were surrounded by Nazis, he plunged into an icy river, leading them to escape. He earned two Purple Hearts and a Bronze Star. Later he graduated with a degree in chemistry from Hofstra and a masters degree in journalism from Syracuse. A lifelong New Yorker, in the mid 1960s he finally left the East Coast's bitter winters to settle in the warm sunshine of Southern California. He was married three times, to Doris Flood, then Sheila McErlean, and finally to Gayle Hallenbeck Stone Lynds. He had two daughters, Katie and Deirdre Lynds, and two step children, Paul and Julia Stone.

Dennis Lynds died at age 81 in 2005. Jack Adrian wrote in *The Financial Times*, "Unusually for a mystery writer – as a breed, they tend to favor things as they are, rather than as they might be – the American author Dennis Lynds, politically, came from left of center. This did not mean he preached bloody revolution. He wrote to entertain." Entertainment was something Lynds never forgot, that and to be generous to his friends.

Obituaries celebrating his work appeared around the globe. In a typical understatement, he commented near the end of his life, "I had a good run." His career had lasted more than fifty years.

The Brass Rainbow
#2 in the Edgar Award–winning Dan Fortune mystery series
by Dennis Lynds
Originally published under the pseudonym Michael Collins

Con artists and call girls, hoods and hippies, and New York City's untouchably wealthy populate this smashing tale of a small-time crook wanted for a murder he swears he didn't commit. The problem lands with

The Brass Rainbow is the second novel featuring Dan Fortune, following the Edgar Award–winning *Act of Fear*. In this one, Fortune goes on the hunt when an uptown blueblood ends up dead and Sammy vanishes. Sammy had always been a loser, and a petty liar, and a magnet for hard luck. Still, Fortune doesn't think he killed the guy. What else can a one-armed detective do, if not help his friends? And Sammy is a friend. Soon Fortune finds himself targeted, and the disappearance of Sammy becomes more puzzling. Is Sammy the killer – or the victim of a frame-up?

Written in the crisp style he helped popularize, the legendary Lynds opens the floodgates to the bygone colorful era of '60s Chelsea – no pricey real estate then, just a teeming Petri dish of hustlers and pigeons and those trying to make a living any way they can. Lynds captures the richness and exposes the underbelly in a tale *The New York Daily News* called, "engrossing."

"The man who won the Mystery Writers of America award … has given readers another exceptional story." – *Parade of Books*

"Skillfully plotted with finely honed suspense." – *New York Times*

"[Lynds] is a writer to watch and above all to read." – Ross Macdonald

"A master of crime fiction." – *Ellery Queen Mystery Magazine*

###

Made in the USA
Monee, IL
11 April 2023